HAIR PEACE

Piers Anthony is the author of over 170 books. His popular series include *Xanth, The Incarnations of Immortality, Chromagic, Geodyssey, Mode, Bio of a Space Tyrant, Adept,* and *Cluster.*

Other books by Piers Anthony from Dreaming Big Publications:

Writer's Retweet
Service Goat
Relationships 6
Relationships 7 (coming soon)

Other books in this series:
Hair Power
Hair Suite

Collaborations by Piers Anthony
and Kenneth Kelly:
Virtue Inverted
Amazon Expedient
Magenta Salvation (coming soon)

HAIR PEACE

The third novella in the Hair Suit series following
Hair Power and *Hair Suite*

Piers Anthony

HAIR PEACE

Copyright © 2017 by Piers Anthony

Cover Art: Macario Hernandez

Editor-in-Chief: Kristi King-Morgan

ISBN-13: 978-1-947381-11-7

Dreaming Big Publications

INTRODUCTION

This is the third novella in the Hair Suit series, following *Hair Power*, where terminally ill Quiti helps an alien hairball and is rewarded with spectacular hair, and *Hair Suite*, which introduces the alien Chip Monks who have similar powers from their chips. Both Hairs and Chips have the power to cure illness such as cancer or AIDS, and to endow their hosts with phenomenal intelligence, handsomeness, and other useful powers. They now occupy their joint embassy in a small city in America, tolerated by global powers because they are both popular and dangerous to cross. They are in touch with galactic civilization via the Worm Web, a network extending across the galaxy and beyond. Don't worry, if you're a new reader; details will be clarified as necessary, though it wouldn't hurt you to go back and read the other two.

CHAPTER 1: HAIR SKIRT

It had quickly become a daily ritual. Quiti emerged from the Hair Suite of the City Hall, garbed in her shining robe, and advanced to the plaza where a throng of ordinary men, women, and children awaited her as if she were a phenomenal celebrity. Which she was, but the experience was still new enough to give her pleasure.

She ranged out with her mind, assessing the noesis, the group intellect. It was positive; there were no haters here, no xenophobes, no lurking assassins. That was a relief. She could nullify a killer, telepathically turning his mind to confusion so that he forgot his mission, but she much preferred not to. Today there was the usual assortment of old and new minds, old being the regulars who came almost every day, new being those who had never been here before. Among the new minds there were some skeptics, but they were not hostile, and they would not be skeptical long. Among the old minds were the supportive older folk, the admiring young women, and the young men who were mentally stripping her naked and taking her to bed. *Not today* she thought to the one with the worst crush on her, and he smiled, appreciating that much of a direct mental contact with her.

"Hi folks!" she called, waving. Informality was the order of the day.

HAIR PEACE

"Hi, Hair Brain!" they clamored back. It was no insult; the Hair Suits were of genius level, though they seldom cared to show it. Instead, they stressed being ordinary folk with some special gifts.

"What can I do for you today?"

"The Hair Skirt!" a thirteen-year-old new boy cried. News of her little show had of course gotten around.

Quiti looked at him. "Does your mother approve of that?"

"She's not here today."

There was general laughter. He was being naughty, but others looked interested.

"Your logic is persuasive," Quiti said. "Hair Skirt it is." She glanced around. "Promise not to tell."

There was a ripple of laughter. They loved her teasing. This reminded her of the start of her manifestation as a hair suit, when she was a twenty-year-old pudgy victim of brain cancer looking for a private place to die. The alien hairball had given her far more than renewed life; it had made her breathtakingly smart and lovely. *Thank you!* she thought to her hair, which was actually a colony of alien creatures. She was their host, but by no means their captive; they made her what she was today. She was vastly more than satisfied. Life, beauty, virtual magic, popularity, power—what more could a girl ask? She was happy to represent them on Earth.

Then she organized her outfit. First, her hair trailed down into a full hair halter, full in the sense of her bosom under it; and a liquidly-flowing hair skirt that looked to be just about to part revealingly when her legs moved under it. In fact, the whole outfit seemed in danger of separating the moment her body moved even slightly too vigorously. Now she had the full attention of the men and boys, and a number of the women and girls too. The boys wanted to catch glimpses of her breasts or thighs, while the girls wanted to see how she avoided giving such glimpses. All part of the naughty tease. Some of the older folk who had seen this dance before were quietly smiling.

Quiti caught a hank of her hair in her left hand and separated it into several taut strands extending from her head to her splayed fingers. Then she used her right hand to pluck the strands, and music sounded in the manner of a harp. It was the melody of a popular song, vibrant, as if issuing from a loudspeaker.

She started the dance. Her hair swirled out from her head and from her bosom, somehow not interfering with her makeshift harp, but without exposing anything: her halter became a concealing cone. It came together at her narrow waist, and flared again around her hips, again without showing anything salacious. Her legs parted, and the hair skirt parted too, in the manner of a grass garment that had no solid material, not quite showing her thighs. She whirled, and the hair lifted in a spreading ring, above and below, but her body was shadowed beneath it.

She whirled harder, and the hair spread into full circles that left no coverage of breasts or hips. But there was nothing to be seen. Those sections of her torso had become invisible. "I don't know how I do it," she sang.

HAIR PEACE

"Making love out of nothing at all." Literally, it seemed. The harp faded out, freeing her hands, but its music continued. Somehow she was playing it without hands, which were disappearing anyway.

Then she made it more obvious. Her hair started fading as she danced, so that it no longer covered her private parts. It spiraled down from her head, past her halter, and went translucent, then transparent, then disappeared entirely. But there was no bosom under it, only empty space. There was a murmur of surprise from the newer part of the audience.

Now her head and upper torso were gone, but her body remained from the waist down. The hair formed into a skirt that extended to her knees, and the knees faded out along with the rest of her legs and feet. Only the skirt itself remained, still dancing as if supported by a vigorous body. The hips jerked to and fro, in time to the music, moving the hidden center of gravity. It was a provocatively sexy display—of nothing at all.

Then faint outlines appeared, as if some celestial hand were sketching the outline of firm legs below, and bouncing breasts above. When the skirt flexed as if moved by a high kick, the outline showed one leg lifting almost to head height, exposing all that was beneath it. Which was nothing but the inside of the skirt. Now the audience murmur was of awe. The eyes of the young men were straining, but simply not finding what they sought. It was pure flirtation, but they were loving it.

It was projected illusion, a function of her telepathy. She touched the minds of the watchers, sending images. It helped that they were willing participants, happy to go along with her suggestions; they could readily have resisted them had their collective mood been negative. She was actually dancing fully clothed in her hair, but delivering the illusion of selective emptiness. Because it was not one person watching, but a hundred or more, she could not do it as thoroughly, but she had learned to aid it with mechanics. She used her magnetic component to divert the rays of light around her limbs and continue beyond uninterrupted, so it never actually interacted with her body. It was another wonderful gift of the hair.

In due course, the solo skirt lengthened and the flimsy outlines of her legs and bosom strengthened, until she was whole again. But so was her outfit, so that nothing private showed. The tease was done, for the moment.

Quiti, maintaining light telepathic contact, became aware of a need. A young woman in the audience, Ola, was here only because another woman she wanted to impress, Pacifa, was here. Ola was a lesbian, and wished she could flash the other lesbian and get her serious attention for a relationship. She was afraid to approach her directly, because lesbians could be as tricky to handle as men. It had to be done correctly; a wrong move could sour it forever. What she really needed was to catch Pacifa's eye so that *she* would approach *Ola*. But how? That was the problem.

Quiti knew the answer. "I need a volunteer," she announced, then gave Ola a mental nudge that

HAIR PEACE

propelled her forward before anyone else moved, to her surprise.

"Thank you," Quiti said. "All you have to do is match my steps. Can you handle that?"

Ola opened her mouth to protest that she couldn't possibly equal Quiti's superlative dancing, let alone match steps and high kicks with her. But Quiti sent another signal, and the young woman shut her mouth and came to stand beside her, emulating her posture. Ola was shapely and pretty in her blouse and skirt, with long dishwater blond hair and delicate slippers: she was a very female female.

"Exactly," Quiti said. She lifted one arm, and Ola did the same, prompted by another mental signal. Then the opposite leg, kicking high enough to show panties, except that somehow nothing quite showed. Ola matched her perfectly.

Telepathy! Ola thought, catching on. Now she knew she was being manipulated like a marionette, and didn't object: she could break free anytime.

Go with the flow, Quiti thought, as Ola's hair seemed to become bright platinum and twice as full, complementing Quiti's suddenly golden tresses. The invisible harp twanged as they went into a high-stepping, hip-thrusting, hair-flinging dance that might have been interesting with one person, but was more than twice as interesting with two perfectly synchronized dancers. It was said that the most beautiful thing in the world was two women making love. This was close to that. They whirled in consummate time, then came together for an intimate swing, and separated for the concluding bow to the audience.

There was vigorous applause. The men loved it, and so did Pacifa, who was amazed. She had seen Ola around, and knew her nature, but had no idea she was capable of such a show. That changed things.

"Isn't she something?" Quiti asked, glancing at Ola. "I couldn't have done it without her." There was more applause.

Ola, nudged by a thought, went to stand beside Pacifa, as if coincidentally. Her performance was done. She looked slightly dazed, as none of this had been deliberate on her part.

Then Quiti proffered another view. The column of her hair descended from crown to toe, with outlines of her head, face, neck, shoulders, breasts, waist, hips, thighs, legs, and feet, all masked beneath the hair but highly suggestive, shaped by the moving tresses. This was the essence of the Hair Dance. The harp music ended.

The audience applauded again, then dissipated, knowing the show was over until tomorrow. Pacifa and Ola departed together, chatting amiably. Quiti smiled, knowing that they were now an item. Ola shot one glance at her, appreciating what she had done.

One boy approached. "Ma'am—" he started hesitantly, but then was tongue-tied by her nearness.

She focused on him, reading his mind. He was Ripley, age sixteen, of generally good character but of course teen horny. He had a ferocious crush on her, but knew it was normal and would pass. His grandfather

HAIR PEACE

was wheelchair-ridden and could not conveniently come to the show without making a scene, and chose not to believe the broadcasts. Ripley wanted very much to persuade Grandpa that he was not imagining things, that Quiti really did become invisible during her dance. He had actually gotten Grandpa to accompany him in the car, but the man refused to leave it for the show. If only Quiti would consent to walk to the car and do just a little magic...

It was a sensible request, considering. She did have a bit of spare time, and the parked car was not far distant. "Yes, Ripley," she said. "Let's go see Grandpa."

The youth was amazed, not by her mind reading, but by her agreement. He had feared rejection, but had forced himself to try. "Yeah," he agreed gratefully.

She took his hand, as that made silent communication feasible. "Show the way, please."

For a moment he was faint, wobbling on his feet. She was holding his hand! His whole arm, up to the shoulder, seemed to be radiating pleasure.

Steady, Ripley, she thought. *It is easier for me to share your thoughts this way. Just walk to the car.*

"Yeah," he repeated. Then he corrected himself. *I mean, yeah. Thanks!* It seemed he was a quick study.

They walked in the right direction. The few people remaining in the area did not notice them, thanks to her gentle diversion of their attention. She also tuned into the boy's surface thoughts, and that was interesting. They passed a young woman, and Ripley's mind flared with pleasure as he gazed at her nicely formed bosom, which jogged slightly with each step she took. Quiti made a private mental note: make sure her bosom jogged similarly when she walked. It had to be just the right amount.

Another girl was walking ahead of them, the youngest of three people, and Ripley's attention was riveted to her flexing bottom beneath her tight, short skirt, as it tuned out others. Quiti had forgotten how fixated young men were on the parts of young women; this was another useful reminder. Quiti could make her body appear ultimately shapely, but that was only part of it; the way it moved was just as important.

The girl was idly tossing and catching a bangle with one hand. Then it bounced off her fingers and dropped to the ground, rolling to a stop behind her. "Oopsy!" she exclaimed as she stopped, turned, and squatted to pick it up, showing firm young cleavage above and smooth inner thighs below.

Ripley almost freaked out as the peek imprinted itself forever on his mind. Then she got the bracelet, rose, turned, and resumed her walk.

Quiti picked up from the girl's mind that she had done it on purpose, not so much to flash Ripley but to verify that Quiti was indeed holding his hand. That, too, was interesting.

They came to the car. An old man was sitting in the passenger seat, looking out the open window. "Hey, Grandpa!" Ripley called. "I brought her! This is Quiti, the Hair Brain!"

Grandpa stared. "And you're holding hands with her? She's a married woman."

HAIR PEACE

"It's an open marriage, Mr. Shylock," Quiti said modestly.

He was surprised. "You know my name?"

She smiled. "I read your mind. It is one of my powers."

"I'll be damned."

"Everything Ripley told you is true," she continued.

He was starting to believe. "Even—?"

"Especially," she said, flashing him with her fine bare breasts as her blouse faded out. It turned out that old men, too, suffered flares of pleasure from such glimpses. Then she leaned forward and kissed his cheek. "It is nice meeting you. Ripley holds you in high regard. He thought you might enjoy meeting me in person."

Mr. Shylock was silent. It was his turn to be overwhelmed. Quiti knew that he would never again belittle his grandson's interests. In fact, he too now had a passing crush on Quiti, and would surely show up at her next show. To support his grandson, of course, no other reason.

Then she dampened her awareness of their thoughts and walked back to the Embassy, alone. They would remember this encounter for a long time.

It was all part of Public Relations, making sure the Hair Suits were held in good regard.

There were people at the Hair Embassy, of course, doing the routine chores that Quiti didn't care to bother with. She was holding the fort alone, as far as Hairs and Chips went, as the others had gone through a Worm Hole and were entertaining galactic tourists with naughty fantasy skits. The only other significant person here at the moment who counted was Idola, a Chip Monk. She was a pretty brown-haired girl, age eleven, the informal girlfriend of Quiti's adopted son Tillo, a twelve-year-old Hair Suit. Quiti was nominally babysitting her, though as a Chip, the girl could certainly take care of herself.

Quiti's mind ranged back in a quick review. Idola was the daughter of her best friend Gena, herself now both a Hair Suit and a Chip Monk, the only one in their group of that kind. In her impetuous youth, Gena had found herself caught, a single mother, and given her baby up in an open adoption, remaining in touch. Now she was married to the adoptive father, a good straight human man, so Idola, by that devious history, was her legal as well as her blood child. Idola had a heavy subject to study for, so was out in a field of flowers with her big British Literature book, determined to get it right.

Quiti's mind ranged out to intercept the mind of the girl because, while the Chips were highly talented, they were not telepathic. She found her, and paused.

Because Idola was not exactly alone.

Joining you, Quiti thought.

Thanks, the girl responded. *There's something odd.*

There was indeed.

CHAPTER 2: LOST CHILD

Idola was sitting on a hillock overlooking a field of flowers, deep in her study of the British poet William Wordsworth. It was for a test, and she hated tests. She had had little interest in poetry of any kind, but since she had acquired her Chip and become phenomenally more intelligent, pretty, clairvoyant, and able to fly, she had discovered virtues in obscure things.

Sometimes she really had to focus on keeping her feet on the ground, because she was trying to come across as a regular garden-variety girl. She had seen from the reaction of strangers to the Hair Suits how distorted things could get when their special powers were too openly displayed. Her classmates knew that she had a connection, but did not know that she had herself become a supernatural creature. They were, of course, watching her; any slip, such as literally flying, would ruin her partial anonymity.

Regardless, she had new interests to indulge, such as ancient poets. Wordsworth had lived from 1770 to 1850—memorization of such dates now came easily to her—had loved a French woman, but lost her when England and France went to war, separating them, and he was poor. Idola related to that, though her family was not poor—not wealthy, but not poor—and she was not separated from her boyfriend. Not by a war or an ocean, at any rate; just by ordinary routine, such as school. She could handle that. The poet was concerned about the French Revolution and the rise of Napoleon, which happened on his watch. She had studied France in another class, so related to that too. He was actually there! So she approached Wordsworth with a recently-opened mind.

All she had to do was select a poem and discuss it knowledgeably in class. In older days, circa last year, she would have picked one of the shortest items in the book, such as maybe "She Dwelt Among the Untrodden Ways," only twelve lines long. It was about a girl few folk knew or loved, concluding, "She lived unknown, and few could know/ When Lucy ceased to be;/ But she is in her grave, and, oh,/ The difference to me!" That got to her; she could have been that girl, who maybe died, she thought, unloved, then was mourned too late. By maybe someone famous like Wordsworth. What a grand way to expire!

But that was then. Now she was a Chip Monk, with enormously broadened horizons. Now she meant to tackle the most challenging poem, "ODE: Intimations of Immortality from Recollections of Early Childhood." Just the title was a challenge! Her problem was not in understanding it herself, but finding a way to describe it to the ordinary children of her class so that they could understand it, when it was frankly well beyond the sixth-grade level.

HAIR PEACE

She was trying her best to continue seeming average, as her classmates did not know of her transformation. Her teacher did, but Mom had had a talk with her that ensured her silence. Mom was good at that sort of thing, buttressing her argument with subtle but persuasive telepathy.

That meant describing the essence of the poem in language anyone could understand. Part of its thesis was that babies came to the mortal world with a suggestion of that immortal realm from which they had just departed. Not that Wordsworth had believed that; he was just invoking the popular mythos for his art. "Not in entire forgetfulness,/ And not in utter nakedness,/ But trailing clouds of glory do we come/ From God, who is our home:/ Heaven lies about us in our infancy!"

Beautiful! But the children were all too likely to take it literally, titter at the nakedness, and look for little clouds; serious allegory was beyond them. Maybe a more concise statement, farther along in the poem: "O joy! That in our embers/ Is something that doth live,/ That nature yet remembers/ What was so fugitive!" But would they understand that this too was figurative; there were no hot embers in anyone's pants? She did not trust them.

Maybe this: "Though nothing can bring back the hour/ Of splendor in the grass, of glory in the flower." But the naughty boys would claim the splendor was a naked woman sunbathing there. Boys were like that. Actually it referred to the blooming of the flower in the grassy field, like the one before her, showing its

19

splendor, its glory, only for an hour or a day before fading, never to be recovered. That was the tragedy of life, that dullness governed except for brilliant moments, and folk just had to make do with what remained. "We will grieve not. Rather find/ Strength in what remains behind." Such as the ordinary plants that produced the flowers in their moments of splendor.

She gazed out across the field of flowers, mourning those that had faded yesterday. What a marvel each one was, yet most of them would die unnoticed and unmourned. Never again would she see a flower without being reminded of its mortality, thanks to the poet's insight.

Then Idola became aware that she was not alone. There was something at the edge of the field, her clairvoyance told her, but she couldn't identify it. It seemed invisible. For that, she would need help. Maybe Aunt Quiti, with her Hair Suit telepathy, could clarify it. Idola remained still, so as not to reveal that she had caught on to the presence in the field, knowing it was no ordinary weed, and set her mind on Contact.

I am here, Quiti thought. *I will read its mind, if it has a mind.*

Quiti merged her telepathy with Idola's clairvoyance; so that it was as if the two of them were a single entity, their mind ranging out across the field, searching out the mystery. They had learned to do that, because they were friends and trusted each other, and because their merged powers were greater than their separate ones. Thus Idola could become telepathic,

HAIR PEACE

temporarily, while Quiti became clairvoyant. Right now that really helped.

They located the oddity; it remained obscure. But Quiti's knowledge was a significant advantage. *That's no regular creature. That's galactic.*

Galactic!

I recognize the traces. Not a species we have encountered before, however, but definitely from a foreign system.

I knew there was something about it, Idola thought. *What's it doing here?*

That's the sixty four million dollar question. Quiti continued to focus, studying the alien. *It's a child.*

A child!

A lost child. A little boy.

That changed things. *Maybe trailing clouds of glory,* Idola thought, with a background of canned laughter.

We have to help it. For Quiti had a motherly streak, for all that she had not yet birthed her own children.

Idola was glad to agree. *How?*

There was the question. *See if we can summon him here.*

"Maybe—" Idola said hesitantly, returning to physical speech so as to use a parallel mode of communication.

"Out with it, girl. Don't make me read your mind."

That was the idea. "I have the clairvoyance, so I know where he is. But I can't actually see him. He's definitely alien."

"But maybe if you can send him a come here directive—"

"I tried," Idola thought. "But he's afraid of me."

"Yes. He's a child. Maybe his mother warned him not to trust strangers."

"Exactly."

"So we need something else," Quiti said.

"But he might trust another mother."

"That's crazy!"

"I do get some crazy notions," Idola agreed. "But if one thing doesn't work, maybe another will."

Quiti sighed. Then she focused. *Alien child. I am someone's mother. Respond to me.*

Idola knew that while Quiti had never birthed a baby, she did have a son: twelve-year-old Tillo, a Hair Suit she and handsome Roque had adopted so he could have a family. That had led to marvelous things, such as Tillo meeting Idola, who was well familiar with the adoption process, who had promptly adopted him as her boyfriend. As a result of that association, Idola had later become a Chip Monk, with powers of her own, and they made a marvelous couple. It was bound to become more impressive once they became hot blooded teens. So Quiti did have the authority of the mother office.

And the alien child did respond. *I sense you.* Not hear or see or feel, because the alien might not have

HAIR PEACE

those senses, but a mind contact was sensing. Definite progress.

"Well, screw me into a socket and turn on the power," Quiti muttered. "It's working!"

"You're so smart," Idola said.

"Cut the crap, girl. It was your idea."

It was good-natured humor, because they were both geniuses, thanks to their alien associations. Fortunately, they really liked each other. Quiti was in many respects the woman Idola wanted to become.

Then Quiti focused again, while Idola tuned in. *Alien child, what is your name?*

Name?

The thing that identifies you as an individual. What does your mother call you?

The answer was a conflux of magnetic currents.

Idola smiled. The kid was after all an alien creature.

"Maybe we can give him a name, for our use," Idola suggested.

"Another crazy yet practical notion. Pick a name."

Idola was at a momentary loss, something that seldom happened to her. "Maybe if we could at least *see* him."

Child, show yourself.

There was a hesitation. Then something vaguely resembling a new plant appeared among the flowers. It was like a stick figure, a metallic column with a single wheel at the base and a cluster of wire loops at the top, forming a figure rather like, yes, an alien flower.

"Flower," Idola said promptly.

PIERS ANTHONY

We will name you Flower, Quiti thought to the alien child. *You will answer to that name, at least while you are on our planet.*

Flower, the child agreed obediently.

Flower, come here.

And, slowly, the sunflower stalk moved toward them, fading in and out as it progressed, as if not quite certain of its orientation.

"Maybe he's not well," Idola said, concerned.

Flower, are you ill? Quiti asked with proper motherly sympathy.

No. Just lost.

But you are fading.

It is hard to maintain the image when I'm strange.

"He means he feels strange on this strange world," Idola said.

Of course it is hard, Quiti agreed supportively. *Where is your mother?*

I don't know! Flower wailed mentally. He was now directly in front of them.

How did you get here without her?

I followed a worm hole, but I forgot to plant a locale, and now I'm lost. He dissolved into mental tears.

"A worm hole," Idola said. They knew about worm holes; they gave easy access to the rest of the universe. "Anyone could get lost."

I am a Hair Suit, Quiti thought, her six-foot tresses flaring like a whirled cape. *Do you know of our kind, Flower? We're Galactics.*

Yes, he agreed faintly.

HAIR PEACE

And my companion is a Chip Monk. Do you know of them?

Yes.

So you know we're real people, not savages.

Yes. That is why I sought you. I thought you might help me.

"That explains why he came to me," Idola said, pleased. "He recognized my galactic aura."

I am going to hug you, Flower. Remember, I'm a mother.

She did not do it physically, but mentally. Her essence, imbued with reassurance, reached out and enclosed the child.

And it worked. Flower settled down, comforted, no longer tearful. He was at this point more child than alien.

Now they were able to get more of the story. Flower's folk were the Ghobots, or Ghost Robots, not held in high regard by other galactics, but generally tolerated. Neither Quiti's Hairs nor Idola's Chips knew of them specifically, but that did not mean they were not legitimate. They traveled around, entertaining the natives of many cultures, generally well received at first. Then, too often, the sentiment turned against them. They had been expelled from their last planet, and were now looking for a new one. Flower had happily joined the search, thinking it a kind of game, and had spied a promising world beyond a worm hole. He had zipped to it, but forgotten to plant his locale, which was marking a spot, rather like blazing a trail. Without that marker, he could not return; he was lost. His mother had, of course, told him repeatedly, always to mark his place, but he was young and made mistakes.

Your mother must be frantic! Quiti thought.

Yes. I'm a bad boy.

Not bad. Just foolish.

Foolish, he agreed, accepting her adult decision.

But there was something else. Idola felt it, and knew that Quiti felt it, too. It was not that the boy was trying to deceive them: he lacked the guile. But something was not completely right about this situation. For one thing, why were the Ghobots first welcomed to a new planet, then rejected? Was there something about them that the natives learned that changed their minds? Why not just talk with them, to negotiate terms of residence and correct the problems? Flower clearly didn't know, but it had to be important.

"We need to know more, before we act," Quiti said. "Suppose you babysit Flower while I go inquire."

"Inquire?"

"I mean to ask the Sorceress. She should know."

"Ah. Of course," Idola agreed. She was familiar with her from their first fantasy adventure, entertaining a galactic audience. The sorceress had been just another actress, but Quiti's later association with her had increased her respect enormously, and she now thought of her as capitalized. It had become a title rather than merely a role.

CHAPTER 3: SORCERESS

Quiti used the miniature wormholes route they had learned from the Chips; these had become familiar in the course of their galactic entertainments. They were essentially cracks in the fabric of the universe that bypassed the normal rules of space travel. Space-time might be considered a huge quilt, endlessly convoluted, folded in on itself, whose flea-like occupants were limited to the decorated surface and were not even aware of its considerable curvature. The cracks thus could connect close spots that seemed impossibly far apart to the fleas. To them, such travel seemed almost magical.

Wormholes ranged in size from stellar to microscopic. The big ones could swallow stars and belch them out in other galaxies. The micros could transport single atoms to quantum obscurities. In between were the traveling ones that could accommodate human-sized folk, transporting them instantly to their termini, where other holes were available for further jumps. They were extremely handy for space travel because they could cover light years in instants.

PIERS ANTHONY

With certain cautions: living creatures were unable to use them, because any live creature that entered a wormhole emerged at the other end dead. They could be used to ship inanimate objects, but the fabric of wormholes was so convoluted that it was impossible to be sure that a given delivery would arrive in the right place. So their preferred use was for messages, though these too had their problems. They could arrive garbled or subtly changed. The Chip Monks had a natural affinity for wormholes and could use them to travel astrally, transporting their conscious spirits but not their bodies. So, in the end, the Hair Suits like Quiti had learned to use their telepathy to fathom the correct wormholes, the ones that went where folk wanted to go, rather than into chaos and limbo. With conscious selection and steering, it was like physical traveling, only without the body.

Quiti parked her physical body, then entered a wormhole and steered her spirit to the planet and abode of the Sorceress, who was actually a sapient alien ribbon fish and galactic actress. She wasn't actually a sorceress; that was merely the role she had played during their first encounter, and she kept the form for Quiti's convenience. How a creature resembling a deep sea snake had achieved human-level intelligence Quiti had no idea; but the Sorceress was herself bemused by the manner a creature resembling a monkey perched on two feet on land had achieved similar status. They had met while playing roles in an animated fantasy adventure, and soon become friends. The Sorceress

HAIR PEACE

admired Quiti's youthful vigor, and Quiti admired her friend's experience and wisdom.

The trail led to the watery planet, then to a particular sea, and finally to a coral-like overhang that was the Sorceress's abode. Quiti emerged in the salty water and assumed the form of—a ribbon fish. "Sorceress!" she called via lateral line pulses. "Are you available?"

"Quiti!" the Sorceress replied as she assumed the form of a human woman. "It is so nice to see you again."

The two faced each other. Quiti made a twisting serpentine wriggle, and the Sorceress formed a facial smile. They enjoyed emulating each other to the extent feasible, though neither form was physical; both were astral projections.

"I have a problem," Quiti said.

"I regret I am unable to eliminate your land monkey nature. You are cursed with it as long as you live."

Quiti laughed. "Not that problem. It's that we have encountered a lost galactic child we think we should help and we need more information."

"Ah. Tell me more."

"He's actually quite sweet, but there's something missing from what he is able to tell us. There's a mystery that makes me wary. That's why I came to you for advice. You have Galactic experience."

"Can you describe him?"

"It is what we call a Ghobot. That is, a ghostly robot."

The Sorceress smiled, knowing this was a form of nonsense. "Form a picture."

Quiti projected an image of Flower.

"That is a /}]+^!" the Sorceress exclaimed, the word cryptic because Quiti's alphabet lacked any equivalent sounds.

"We call him Flower, because he vaguely resembles, well, a sunflower with a wheel at the base of his stalk."

"That will do. I am checking my Wormpedia. This may be an unfortunate encounter."

Quiti was alarmed. "Is that species dangerous?"

"Not exactly. But there's a fair prospect of this association becoming awkward to the point of danger, to you and the child alike."

"Flower certainly seems harmless."

The Sorceress pondered. "How shall I phrase this? Do you have peoples who are discriminated against by others? Even oppressed without proper reason?"

"You mean like the Jews or Gypsies?"

"Perhaps. Tell me more about them."

"Well, the Jews were the source of two of the greatest other religions on Earth, the Christians and the Muslims, yet they are widely distrusted for reasons that generally turn out to be false. The Gypsies have been treated similarly. In fact the Nazis—"

"The whats?"

"The Nazi party came to rule Germany in our 1930s. They practiced genocide in the name of improving our planet's racial composition. As I understand it, they put four groups into their death

HAIR PEACE

camps for extermination: the Jews, the Gypsies, the gays—"

"The whats?"

"The gays. Homosexuals. Those who prefer to romance their own gender."

The Sorceress was surprised. "This is a crime?"

"To some. In some regions the penalty for being gay is death."

"Our cultures do differ."

Quiti resumed the thread. "The fourth category was enemy prisoners, especially the Russians. All four groups were being killed wholesale. The Nazis were by no means the only ones who killed minorities; it's endemic in our world."

"And in some galactic worlds," the Sorceress said grimly. "This does not simplify the problem of your lost child."

"You think Earth would turn against his kind?"

"Yes. The history is there."

Quiti was uncomfortable. "We are slowly liberalizing. We do not persecute minorities so much any more, at least in America."

"Surely not," the Sorceress agreed supportively, though she might have had another opinion. "The Gypsies. Tell me more about them."

"The story is that they came originally from India. That perhaps Alexander the Great imported them to Romania for labor, but they retained their own culture. That sort of separated them from the local population, the way the Jews insistence on maintaining their own form of worship did for them. Then they were turned loose and had to flee to other nations. They called themselves Gypsies, that is, from the country of Egypt, so as to conceal where they were actually from. They were really more like a race unto themselves, with a separate culture. They would put on shows, do divination, mix love potions and so on, to make their living. They could dance intricately well, and I understand their women could be quite sexy, which helped bring in money. But they were generally in bad report and forced to move on, so they truly had no permanent home."

The Sorceress nodded, a mannerism she had practiced; she was excellent at emulating the human nuances. "They seem to be a fair model for the situation of your lost child. Originally, these people you call Ghobots are typically welcomed to a new world, and become quite popular there, like your Gypsies with their merriment and pretty dancing girls. But after a time their welcome cools, and finally they are driven from the world. That is surely why they are looking for a new one."

"But why? Why welcome them, then unwelcome them?"

"That is the mystery. The natives of a number of worlds have been questioned, according to the Wormpedia, but have been canny in their answers, with demonstrably false reasons, as if they don't really want to give their true reasons. I fear it could be the same on Earth."

"How can we find out the true reasons, if they're not simply bigots?"

HAIR PEACE

"There may be a way, but it may be uncomfortable."

"This whole cruel mystery is uncomfortable!"

"Then try this," the Sorceress said. "Remember, you can vacate at any point; you do not have to participate beyond your comfort level."

"I can handle a recording," Quiti said, unconcerned.

"This one may be more difficult than you are accustomed to. There are elements that run counter to your culture."

"I can handle it," Quiti said, dismissively.

"You are sure?"

"Sure I'm sure." In later retrospect, Quiti would remember her friend's caution, and resolve to be more sensitive to it. She had not been nearly as well prepared as she supposed.

The Sorceress did not argue further. She brought out a small box containing a pebble. She set the little stone on the floor of the sea. "Gaze on this."

Quiti swam down to its level and eyed the thing. There was a complex array of colors on its surface. As she looked closer, the colors seemed to rise from it in intricate patterns that danced in the water like self-willed ripples. Intrigued, she studied them more closely.

Then the colors swirled larger, enclosing her, and she found herself as a human child in a pretty yellow dress. What was this? Then she realized that her mind was interpreting the signals on its own terms. She was a Ghobot child presented as the mind of the reader saw her, in this case herself, so as to connect without undue confusion. How could she really relate to a creature fashioned from magnetism and iron filings? But with appropriate translation, she was able to see the essence, if not the incidental detail.

"What am I supposed to do?" she inquired somewhat plaintively. It was not actual verbal speech, but magnetic pulses that conveyed the meaning.

"You will dance, dear, as we have taught you. You know how to do it."

"Yes!" she agreed, relieved. She did know how to dance, including the sexy moves, and when she came of age she hoped to be able to wow men into tossing money at her so she could help sustain her family, exactly as the big girls did. It was the Gypsy way. The Ghobot way, but Gypsy was the Earthly approximation.

"If we are fortunate, that will suffice," her mother said, a trifle warily.

"I will dance really well, mama," she promised. "You will be proud of me."

"But we are not always fortunate," her mother said. "In that case, we make do the best we can. This too you must learn."

"I'll do my best."

"There has been a request for an innocent child. You are that." Why did the woman seem sad? "To dance alone for a man."

"I can do it," Quiti insisted stoutly. "In public or alone, with others or by myself. Whatever is needed." She was proud of her dancing ability and liked showing it off.

HAIR PEACE

"Use your best judgment. Remember, we want to please our clients, but there are limits."

"Whatever dance he wants, I'll do. I know them all."

"If you find you can't handle it, break it off and depart," her mother said. "We do need the money, but—"

"Okay, okay," Quiti said impatiently. Adults could temporize forever.

"Wait here," her mother said, showing her to a private chamber. "He will come to you soon."

The client arrived. He was a jolly older man, a bit stout but healthy. "Well, hello little girl!" he exclaimed as he sat on the comfortable chair. "Aren't you the pretty one!"

"Thank you," Quiti said, forcing a cute blush. She knew she was pretty, especially in this outfit, but had a role to play. Children were cutest when innocent.

"What is your name, child?"

"Quiti." Again, her interpretation of the original.

"Delightful," he murmured. "Show me your best dance."

Quiti happily flung herself into a solo show, stepping smartly, whirling so that her hair and skirt flung out, kicking her feet high so as to flash her thighs. She knew that when she was a big girl that would be really sexy. For now, she was satisfied to know that she had it down perfectly.

"Marvelous," he said when she finished.

"Thank you." She was pleased herself, as she breathed a little harder from the effort. That, too, would count for more when she had a quivering bosom to rise and fall.

"Now can you do it again, without your panties?"

Without? That was curious, but if that was what he wanted, why not? Sometimes they even did naked dances. She had practiced every kind of variant. If he thought this was a special challenge, she would handle it. She removed her panties and set them aside, then did the dance again, aware that now the high kicks showed her unfurred cleft.

He watched intently throughout, as if it were phenomenally compelling, though he had just seen the dance. "Terrific! You dance really well, Quiti, and you have nice legs."

"Thank you," she repeated, blushing again. She was glad she was making a good impression.

"Now come sit on my lap."

That was easy. This, too, was a part of some dances. She went to sit on his lap, her bottom bare under the skirt.

He ran his hands over her legs, gently stroking them. "Yes, really nice."

Why was he complimenting her? She knew her legs were nothing special.

Then one finger tickled her crotch. She stifled a giggle. Sometimes she had played tickle games with other children, seeing who could make whom laugh first. But this was generally not a game adults were interested in.

HAIR PEACE

He squeezed her cleft, then used his fingers to open it wide. "Do you know what I would like to do next?"

Then she caught on. He was thinking of sex. She knew what sex was, having seen it performed by adults. "I am underage for that."

"My dear, there is no age limit for your kind, for anything. It is part of your appeal."

For her kind. Now she knew how he truly regarded her. As a member of an inferior species. Civilized rules did not apply to such folk. "My appeal?"

"The young can be especially titillating, when they are pretty, like you."

She had been warned that some men liked women really young. Before they were women, even. She had heard stories. "I have never done it." That was true. "I wouldn't know what to do." That was false: she knew exactly what went where. "I don't want to disappoint you." True again. She simply lacked the evocative equipment of a grown woman, such as breasts.

"You won't disappoint me. Will you do it?" His finger stroked the length of her cleft, stirring an interesting feeling.

He had to have her agreement, so it wouldn't be rape. If she balked, the session would be over, and there would be a bad report. "Maybe," she temporized.

"Let me slide my pants down."

She got off his lap and waited while he did that, revealing his standing member. Now there was no question: when a member stood, it wanted entry.

"Come sit on me again, Quiti. I think you know how."

She did know. It was one of the standard positions, where the woman had nominal control. No force, by definition. There might not be an applicable age limit, but it had to be voluntary, and thus not rape. He wanted her to fit his member into the hole in her cleft and slowly take it inside her body. It might be uncomfortable, but it could be done; the hole expanded to accommodate it.

This was the point where her mother had told her to depart if she couldn't handle it. When she discovered what the man really wanted of her. But that would be failure, and it was not penetration but failure she couldn't handle.

"You do want to do it, don't you?" he asked. It was no question; it was a threat. She had to say that it was her choice. Otherwise, her "dance" was over, and there would be a black mark against both her and her family that could put them into poverty. She wanted to protect her family.

"Yes," she whispered. That was a partial truth.

"You Gypsy girls like doing it."

"Yes." They both knew it was a lie, but a necessary one.

"Come sit," he repeated.

She got back on his lap, then pretty much blanked out on what followed.

When the man departed, her mother looked at her. "You pleased him. He paid a nice bonus."

HAIR PEACE

That was the tip-off: the bonus. She was hurting, physically and emotionally, but she knew she must not say so. "He liked my dance."

Her mother nodded, understanding perfectly. "You used your judgment."

"Yes."

"You did what was necessary. That is all that needs to be known."

"Yes. I danced very well for him."

"You're a good girl. Now go clean up and rest."

Good girl? She was a child prostitute! But this was merely another aspect of her loss of innocence: not the uncomfortable sex, but learning to be a skillful liar. She knew her mother did not like this reality but had no more choice than Quiti did. What good was innocence if they starved to death?

She went to the bathroom and washed out the blood and goo. She knew she would soon heal, and it would not be as difficult in future times. She had to admit that the man had been as gentle as he could manage, letting her take it in her own time and manner. He had been a good client, in that respect. She appreciated that. He, too, was locked into the quiet requirements of his culture, where his particular passion could not be advertised. He, too, would admit only to seeing her dance. It was part of the protocol, a conspiracy of silence by all parties.

She realized, now, that she had been carefully prepared for this throughout her innocence. It had not been coincidence that she had seen adults perform sex in different ways; that she had seen the processes of seduction, the motions, the looks, the words. She had been educated in the ways that counted, without realizing it, so that her overall innocence was preserved. Setting her up for this moment. Because innocence was the single most valuable quality a girl had, and once it was lost it could never be recovered.

In the evening her mother came to her. "Are you angry, dear?" Because her mother knew she had figured it out.

"Furious," she said. "But not at you. I know you had to use your judgment too, and make a difficult choice."

"You do understand. That bonus was huge: it will pay our way for a month. But it was not just for money I did it."

"It was because you had to teach me how to keep a secret," Quiti said. "And how to be a successful Gypsy."

"Exactly. I learned similarly, at your age."

Then they hugged each other, and cried a little.

Quiti became quite popular as a child dancer, because of her prettiness and the skill of her performance, and contributed handsomely to her clan's welfare. Police did not raid them, though sometimes there was cause, because one of the clients she danced for was connected, and she was known to be absolutely safe with a secret.

Then she grew breasts, so that stage of her life was over. She moved on to a new clientele, those who liked their girls young but not that young, and

HAIR PEACE

continued to do well. Meanwhile, she developed expertise in their other services.

One man watched her dance, then broached a different matter. "Our interaction is private," he said.

"Yes. Nothing that is said or done here will be spoken of elsewhere." Not directly, anyway.

"I am looking for something other than sex."

She took it in stride. She had no official position to handle anything other than dancing, but that was the point: there was no record of their dialogue. He was officially just here for slightly illicit sex. "What is the venue?"

"I owe money to a person. I am ready to pay, but the debt is illicit and may not be paid openly. Can you help me?"

"Yes. You understand that we must verify that you are not a shill for the police."

Silently he handed her his ID card. She took her spot scanner and recorded it. He was clean, at least in that respect. She returned the card. "How much money, to what person?"

He named the figure and the person.

"There is a fee of five percent."

He handed her the fee in cash.

"Go down to our casino. Play roulette. At first, you will win small amounts. Then bet the large amount, in several installments. You will lose. The money will be deposited in that person's account without attribution. You need have no further communication with him. He will know the debt is acquitted."

"Thank you. I am relieved." Then he paused.

"Yes?"

"I did not come here for sex. But I think now I would like to have it, in celebration of my relief at handling a difficult matter. Is that still an option?"

"It is part of the dance you paid for. Nothing else happened here." She threw off her dress and came at him naked. In moments, they were in the throes of it. It was almost fun for her, because his passion was in some respects like love.

In another instance, she accepted a small box of potent drugs to be delivered anonymously to a certain party, then sealed the deal with more sex. Some Gypsy women merely handled those other matters, but Quiti was too pretty for that. The clients always wanted the sex too.

When the occasion to marry came, she had no trouble landing the man she wanted. He had been a handsome boy whore, and had risen through the ranks as she had. They were equivalently skilled in their trades and understood each other perfectly.

Time passed in a seeming moment. Now Quiti was an administrator in the clan, sending her virgin daughter to her first private dance. She ached privately for the girl's coming loss of innocence, but it had to be done.

Another moment, and it was her granddaughter's innocence at stake. That was almost as hard to bear.

Then, as a senior executive, she had to cast her vote in a key decision. Things were slowly turning bad, as a new planetary administration came to power and labored to reform the corruption of the old, and the

HAIR PEACE

welcome of the clan on this planet was rapidly eroding. It was considered to be part of the old order, and therefore evil. Meanwhile, things were happening as vigilantes got into the act and were not curbed. The climate was becoming bleak.

Should they seek another world? She thought they should, but the vote went against her, as too many of the other leaders had too many ties to this world and did not want to give them up. It was a bad decision. Covert prejudice flowered into open hostility, as the Gypsies were blamed for all manner of societal ills. It didn't matter that the Gypsies were not guilty: the point was to take their frustration out on a convenient minority. Blaming minorities had one huge advantage: they could not fight back effectively. Soon they were being hunted down and caged in concentration camps. Her husband was killed, her children and grandchildren died fighting, and she survived as much by luck as by skill. She could not escape the planet, but did record her story as a warner for whoso would be warned. She sent it via Worm to other tribes, then planned to drink the final potion. Her day was done.

And to you, Quiti, she thought. *I thank you for your interest, though you are not one of us. Please do what you can. We do need your help.*

Quiti came out of it as the colors swirled back into the stone. "Oh, my," she murmured.

"It does have its moments," the Sorceress agreed.

"She was aware of me! But she's dead."

"That is illusion. It is a to-all-parties message, personalized by category and user, addressed to the unknown reader. But it is oddly effective."

"It is indeed," Quiti agreed. "I am not a Gypsy nor a Ghobot, but I feel for her and by extension for them. If this is what Flower's folk face, I do have to try to help them."

"How?"

"Maybe by inviting them to Earth?"

"Where in two generations they will be hounded and slaughtered as your Gypsies were?"

That set Quiti back. She did not want to be responsible for the kind of mischief she had seen in the recording. But neither did she want to stand idly by as a species was driven to extinction. "What would you recommend?"

"First we need to understand exactly what it is that causes them to be ultimately rejected. It is not precisely what the interpretations of the listeners may suppose."

"Not really young sex or banned gambling or untested drugs, maybe, but they could be part of it," Quiti agreed. "The Gypsies are providing services that are in demand but not officially approved."

"Which eventually gets them in trouble," the Sorceress agreed. "But I suspect there is more to it than that."

"There must be. We need to know precisely what, so we know whether we can handle it."

"Exactly."

HAIR PEACE

"How can I find out, when official channels are obscure?"

"I believe you need to interview your lost child."

"But he's innocent. He doesn't know."

"Innocent in the manner your girl child was in the recording. He surely has seen much, as it seems to be their policy to educate their children in preparation for what they will face in the future, even if they don't yet properly fathom the implications. There should be things you can glean with adult understanding even if he can't see them."

Quiti nodded, appreciating the thoroughness of what she had seen in the recording. "There should be. I'll go have another talk with him."

"Perhaps you should bring in Gena, your more mature friend."

"Gena!" Quiti exclaimed. "Yes! Not only that, but she is both Hair and Chip, with a truly broadened perspective, and she can dream the future. She can figure it out if anyone can." Then she paused, remembering. "But Gena is tied up in one of our Galactic Fantasy productions at the moment. That's how we pay *our* way."

"Not so. She just finished her role there, ahead of the others, and will return to Earth about the time you do."

Quiti was surprised. "How do you know that?"

"I checked around while you were romancing the stone."

Oh. Of course. Why should the Sorceress twiddle her thumbs (or whatever) while Quiti zoned out on the recording? "Thank you so much. This may be our key. I shall hurry home."

"It is always a pleasure to dialogue with you."

"Oh, Sorceress, I would kiss you if there were any feasible way to do it."

"Air kisses, one of your kind's mannerisms I have learned." The Sorceress kissed her own formed fingers and wafted them gently toward Quiti.

Quiti returned the equivalent gesture in ribbon fish terms, then took her wormhole home. She certainly had a lot to think about, and a lot more to learn. She was excited by the prospect.

CHAPTER 4: GHOBOT

In fact, Gena had preceded her, and was in the process of meeting Flower. It was clear that he took to her immediately, perhaps because she was a real mother, and a galactic twice over, being both a Hair Suit and a Chip Monk, although of fairly recent vintage. She had six-foot long hair just like Quiti's own, by no coincidence, brown eyes, and was a shapely woman of 33. The hair was because Quiti had transferred half of hers, and now both halves were filling out into full complements.

Idola saw Quiti's arrival, in the form of the animation of her formerly unconscious body. "Mom's handling it," she said brightly. "Hope you have news."

"I have some," Quiti said cautiously, uncertain how much she should say in Flower's presence. "Maybe I should talk with Gena while you and Flower get to know each other better." She sent a thought to their minds to indicate she had good reason.

"Okay," Idola said. "Let me show you around the embassy, Flower." She took the boy out of the room.

"Something significant?" Gena asked when they were alone, mind shields up for privacy. They had first met when Quiti was fleeing her neighborhood, to

47

escape undue investigation into her new powers, and Quiti had gotten privacy by riding with Gena in Gena's long-haul rig. They had been close friends ever since.

"Let's touch hair." They were both telepathic, thanks to the hair, but closer was better, and actual touch, hair to hair, enabled an instant complete gigabit transfer. That way Gena would immediately know Quiti's full experience.

They leaned toward each other until their hair touched. There was no electric tingle, but Quiti felt Gena's acceptance. Then they straightened up.

"Wow," Gena said, sitting down. "Of course it wasn't necessarily sexual, but it was equivalent."

"Loss of innocence," Quiti agreed. "You must decide whether you want to share this with Idola."

"Oh, she can handle it. Chips don't have telepathy, but I share with her, so she knows what's on every man's mind. She remains virginal by choice, not ignorance."

"As did the Ghobot girl, until her choice was forced."

"She used her best judgment, as will my daughter." She smiled faintly. "But of course Ghobot culture differs from ours: I don't expect Idola to follow that course."

Quiti believed that, knowing Idola, who was one savvy girl and a perfect match for Quiti's son Tillo. So they were still children; but they were also Chip and Hair children, quite another matter.

"The Ghobots have something that others want as much as they do money or sex," Quiti said. "But I

HAIR PEACE

don't think it is either of those. Until we figure it out, we really don't know how to help Flower."

"We're probably best off simply returning him to his folks and exiting the scene without further involvement."

"I believe that was the Sorceress's sentiment."

The older woman met her gaze. "But she knew you would not leave it at that."

"Why do you remind me of the Sorceress?"

Gena laughed. "Why don't I hold down the fort here, while you and Idola take Flower on a broader tour and quietly discover his capacities? Then we'll have a better notion how to proceed."

"Done," Quiti agreed. She liked the girl and was happy to work with her, and she was really curious about the Ghobots.

Quiti and Idola took Flower back to the field. "Now the blazes," Quiti said. "Can you show us exactly how they work, Flower?" She was talking aloud while projecting the focused thought to him.

The Ghobot child brightened momentarily, his equivalent of a smile. Then he walked, in his fashion, about a hundred feet, while they paced him on either side. Then he disappeared.

What?

They both looked around. There was Flower, back at the starting point. He had instantly and silently jumped there.

"This smells like teleportation," Quiti said. That was interesting indeed.

"Unless we suddenly blanked out for a minute while he walked back."

Quiti looked at her watch, noting the time to the second. Then she beckoned Flower.

He disappeared from the distance and reappeared beside them. *You asked to see the blazes work,* he reminded them. *So I jumped back to the one I set.*

No time had passed. They had not blanked out. "So we did," Quiti said. "And so you did. That was very nice, Flower. We can't do that."

Hairs and Chips can't blaze, he agreed. *But Hairs can read thoughts and Chips can read regions.* He meant telepathy and clairvoyance.

"That we can," Quiti agreed. "Each species has its own talents. When we work together we accomplish more than we do alone."

Can I go home now?

He was homesick, of course. "Not yet, but soon. We understand that there are hostile species on the Worm Web, and we believe we can do a better job of returning you safely if we understand you and your kind better."

I guess. He seemed to be impatient with adult caution, as children tended to be.

Idola spoke. "When you do a favor for citizens of your world who are not Ghobots, what do you do? Do you take them on blaze jumps?"

No.

"Why not?"

We can do it only for ourselves.

HAIR PEACE

The girl was getting somewhere. "So what do you do for them?"

We emote.

Quiti exchanged a blank look with Idola. "You make a show of emotion?" Quiti asked.

No, we enhance it.

"Remember, we are not Ghobots," Idola said. "We don't understand everything you do. Can you show us how to emote, your way?"

I guess. But nothing happened. They had asked him a question, not told him to do something. As a child he lacked some of the context adults routinely applied.

"How can we emote?" Quiti asked.

Maybe with a game.

Another blank look. Then Idola came to the rescue again. "A game. Like maybe tick-tack-toe?"

I guess. He clearly did not know the game.

Quiti got a notion. "I will play it with Idola. Can you make us emote?"

One of you.

'Me," Idola said.

You, he agreed, moving close to her.

Were they getting somewhere? They cleared a place on the field so as to have a patch of dirt. Quiti drew a plot of four lines making nine spaces. Idola made the first move, putting an X in the center. Quiti put an O in a corner. "Oh, this is exciting!" Idola exclaimed.

Nothing like a little drama for a little game. When properly played, the game always ended in a draw. But, curious, Quiti played to lose, and soon Idola had three X's in a row. "OOO!" she exclaimed jubilantly, jumping up and down. "I won! I won!"

She was an exuberant girl, but this was too exaggerated, especially since she had to know Quiti had let her win. Then she sobered and looked at Quiti. "Do it for her next," she said.

Flower moved from her to Quiti.

Do what? But Quiti said nothing. Instead she smoothed out the board, made new lines, and put her O in the center. This time Idola played to lose.

Quiti won, and suddenly was totally thrilled. "I won!" she cried, dancing much as Idola had. She had not had joy like this in a long time.

"It's the feeling," Idola said.

Then Quiti caught on. "Emotion," she said. "He enhances emotion. So little victories become phenomenal emotional rides."

"He emotes us," Idola agreed.

They played more games, this time enhancing the losers, and discovered utter dejection. It was as though every tiny feeling was magnified to a giant feeling. This was true even though they knew the effect was artificial.

"It's like a drug high," Quiti said. "Only without the drug."

"And no crashing after," Idola said. "When it stops, it stops without consequence."

Quiti faced Flower. "You have shown us the enhancement of joy and sadness. Can you do other feelings?"

Yes, if I know what feelings.

HAIR PEACE

They discussed it with him, and concluded that though he was not telepathic, he could perceive and affect brain waves, tweaking them to make particular wavelengths stronger. He did not share the feelings himself, but did perceive their effects, and could further enhance them when he oriented on the right ones. He was feeling his way, as it were, but it was effective.

"Think what he could do for an orgasm," Quiti murmured.

"Wow," Idola agreed. "Sexual orbit!"

Oops! "I forgot you are a child," Quiti said, embarrassed.

"A child whose mother has educated her on what counts," Idola said. "She sent me an orgasm so I would know it when I found it."

Oh. With telepathy there were very few secrets, especially when a mother was educating her daughter to be knowledgeable, as was the case with the Ghobot recording. "Similar enhancement during sex could rapidly addict a person."

"Maybe we're getting a handle on what gets the Ghobots into trouble," Idola said. "They're like drug dealers."

"Can't get rid of the market, so have to get rid of the dealers," Quiti said. "Which doesn't really solve the problem, but it makes it look as if the authorities are doing something."

"Let's try something else," Idola said. "Just in case we don't have it nailed yet."

"Good thought. Something really boring, to see how it makes it interesting."

"Baseball. I hate it."

"Oh, do you? I always liked it. Softball, at least."
Quiti remembered playing with the boys, who had
treated her courteously.

"You have to wait and wait for every ball and
every strike. It's dull as school. Even the popcorn and
soda gets to taste like warm poop and piss."

"Baseball it is," Quiti agreed, smiling. "I believe
the local third tier team has a game this afternoon. We'll
go see it, and take turns getting thrilled."

Idola grimaced. "If emoting can make me like the
Sad Butts, it's a super winner."

They returned to the embassy to let Gena know,
then went off to the game. They used Quiti's car, which
was a battered old jalopy with scrapes on its paint and
smudges on its glass: what a poor girl could afford,
clearly no prize. She called it Carmen, as in the operatic
"If Carmen loves you, that's the end of you." What did
not show was that it was thoroughly armored, bullet
and beam proof, with invulnerable tires, and could do a
hundred and fifty miles an hour if there was a track for
it. If any unauthorized person entered it, the doors
would lock and the seat belt would snap into place to
restrain him while a signal went out to alert Quiti.
Carmen loved intruders, and it was the end of them.

Idola, of course, was no intruder. In fact if she
were ever in trouble, such as being chased by a bully
(not that she couldn't readily handle a bully, using her
Chip powers), she could dive in and say "Carmen, help
me!" and it would. Carmen was attuned to Hairs and
Chips and ready to serve them.

HAIR PEACE

But at the moment they were simply driving to the game inconspicuously. Quiti did not even have to use her telepathy to discourage curiosity: Carmen was inherently ignorable.

What is this? Flower inquired, amazed when the vehicle started to move.

"It's a car," Idola explained. "The regular folk of this planet can't teleport the way you can or fly the way we can, so they use powered vehicles. We use it so we won't seem different from them."

We do that too. We hide among the natives.

"Close enough," Idola agreed. Flower wasn't belted, having no beltable anatomy; she was holding him on her lap.

They parked in the partly-filled stadium lot and went in for tickets and the game. Idola carried Flower, who was now invisible. It wasn't that they were sneaking in a spectator, it was that it might be extremely awkward to explain him to an official. They found their seats and settled in to watch.

The Star Bucks, nicknamed Sad Butts, were in their usual feculent fettle, seemingly unable to hit the easiest pitch or catch a fly ball after two bounces. They were losing badly, which was par for their course. But that was hardly the point of this trio's attendance.

Idola took her turn first, emoted by Flower. "Wow!" she breathed as a strike whizzed past the somnambulant Butts batter. "What a pose!"

She was admiring the posture of the player? Well, he was a halfway handsome man and the girl did notice such things.

Then the batter swung and actually hit a little pop fly. "What a marvel!" Idola said, impressed. "The height, the placement."

"I could do better than that," Quiti grumped. "Without Hair enhancement, I mean."

The ball was easily caught for the out. "Such magnificent form," Idola said.

"Give me that emote," Quiti snapped, and Flower moved over.

The next batter struck out. "What phenomenal form," Quiti exclaimed, admiring the activity, while Idola groaned. Their roles had changed, and Quiti was truly impressed by the man's swings; Idola wasn't.

They watched more of the sorry game, alternately thrilled and appalled, depending on who had the emote and whether it was set for positive or negative. There was no question of its effectiveness.

Then Idola perked up as if listening. "People are approaching Carmen. They look like carjackers." It was her clairvoyance, which was oriented on the car.

"Lotsa luck with that!" Quiti said. "Carmen will eat them for dinner."

"I just thought—"

Quiti read her thought. "You're right! Let's try it."

They exited the game early and made their way to the parking lot. Three men were looking at the car, suspicious because it was such an obvious if lowly target. Quiti hardly needed to read their minds to know that.

HAIR PEACE

"Flower, I'm going to tune in those three men," Quiti said. "Can you change their brain waves with my guidance?"

He agreed, not familiar with this process, but willing to try.

She made a close picture of the three heads with their radiating brain waves. Such waves were not visible to ordinary folk, but her telepathy made them appear as wavy lines. "Amplify Fear."

Flower focused, orienting, finding the right waves, strengthening them.

Suddenly the men cried out in alarm and fled in terror.

"Bingo!" Idola exclaimed, watching them go.

"I think we're a team," Quiti said, gratified.

"My clairvoyance, your projective telepathy, Flower's emote," Idola agreed. "We got it together."

Later, back at the embassy, they reported to Gena. "So it is the emoting you think does it?" she asked.

"Yes. When it is positive, any minor little success is thrilling," Quiti said.

"And when it is negative, any little lapse can make you feel suicidal," Idola said.

"So of course clients take the positive emotions," Gena said. "And are soon addicted to them. Until they become useless to society, just staying forever high on emotion. And the only politically convenient way to stop it is to get rid of the Ghobots. They become the scapegoats for the base appetites of planetary citizens."

"That's the way we see it," Quiti agreed.

There was a brief silence.

"Flower has been with us a while," Gena said. "Has he eaten?"

Quiti and Idola exchanged another glance. "We never thought of that," Quiti confessed, embarrassed. "We could have gotten him popcorn at the game."

"Does he eat popcorn?" Idola asked.

"He's a growing child," Gena said. "He must be hungry."

"He must be," Quiti agreed weakly.

Gena addressed Flower. "What do you eat, Flower?"

Eat?

It turned out, with further questioning, that Ghobots did not eat solid foods. They were creatures of energy. Their cores were intense magnetic fluxes, from which they reached out magnetically to grasp not just iron filings but almost any loose substance and form it into the ghostly semblance of a body. They got their energy from limited nuclear fusion, one atom at a time, merging four hydrogen atoms into one helium atom, the same process that powered the sun and stars. All they needed was a local supply of hydrogen, and Earth's atmosphere provided plenty of that. Their waste product was pure helium, harmless in this context.

"Cold fusion!" Quiti exclaimed. "The breakthrough of the century!"

"I think not," Gena said. "This is strictly small scale. The magnetic flux is so strong in that limited region of the Ghobot core that fusion can be forced. Earth has no technology to match that. Best not even to mention it, lest the greed-heads try to take him apart."

HAIR PEACE

Quiti had to agree. Politicians tended to be immune to the realities of science. "Still, it means they are physically harmless. They could come to Earth."

"You are considering bringing the fugitive Ghobots here? When you know they'll soon be anathema because of emote addiction?"

"I'm working on that," Quiti said. "But first we have to return Flower to his folks. That should take only an hour or so, via the Worm Web."

"Maybe," Gena agreed cautiously.

CHAPTER 5: WORM WOOD

"Now remember, Flower," Quiti said as they made ready to travel. "You are a creature of the Worm Web, so your whole body is there. But we are mostly physical creatures, and we have to leave our bodies behind, sleeping. We will be with you in spirit only, more apparent than real. If something happens to us, we will revert back to our physical bodies, leaving you behind. But we want to stay with you, to help guide you to your family. Once you are safely home, then we can depart."

It is like that when the natives of our planet travel, Flower agreed.

"You may be more familiar with the Worm routes of your region than we are. Do let us know if there is something that might mess us up."

I will, mama Hair, he promised.

"Can you sniff out your own route here? I know you can't just jump to it, but is there a trace left as you pass?"

Yes.

"So we can follow it back to where you left your mother."

Yes.

HAIR PEACE

"Then let's go." Quiti took Idola's hand as they leaned back comfortably in their easy chairs. With their free hands they touched Flower, making sure they would travel together.

"'Bye, mom," Idola said as Quiti's telepathy encompassed her and Flower.

Then they focused on the wormholes. It was like diving into a rushing river with many diversions. Idola located the tangled pattern of them clairvoyantly. Quiti telepathically zeroed in on the hole that took them most directly into the main network, avoiding the curls, gaps, and dead ends of the others. It was the telepathy that made this kind of travel feasible: without it Idola would have been in trouble, being able to "see" only one hole at a time beyond the surface pattern. This coordination unified them as an effective traveling entity.

She felt Flower's admiring awareness. The Ghobots had neither clairvoyance nor telepathy, but here in the embrace of her mind he was sharing both.

They came into an annex with several passages leading outward. This was the way Quiti's mind interpreted the nexus to make it reasonably familiar and navigable. "Which direction did you come from, Flower?"

Now the Ghobot appeared in his natural guise, as a stick figured ghostly robot. He sniffed. "That way," he said, pointing. Here on the Worm Web he seemed physical, and could talk in the way they did, or at least like a telephone.

They took that passage. It opened out into a lovely scenic vista. A valley between mountains was covered with handsome pine trees, with puffy white clouds drifting above. This, too, was purely interpretation, but it would do.

They walked along a path through the forest. A soft scented breeze wafted their hair back. It was very nice, but it was mostly illusion. They were moving electronically along the crevices in space-time that were the Worm Web.

They came to an intersection of two trails, and paused. Their original one continued on through the forest, while the other seemed to come from the top of a mountain and wend its way down toward a pond or lake. Both were established worm crevices regularly used by web travelers; the scenic adornments, however interpreted, marked them as usable rather than spurious. "That one," Flower said, pointing toward the pond.

They turned to follow it. As they approached the water, Flower hesitated, then stepped back. "Bad," he said.

"What is it?" Quiti asked.

"I think it's a Worm."

Quiti laughed. "Well, this is the Worm Web." She realized that while on Earth the worms made the wormholes, in the Web the holes preceded the worms, who must have evolved to use them.

"Trouble," Flower said, frightened.

"We'd better pause to figure this out," Quiti said to Idola. They had not yet seen the Worm, but if it was dangerous they needed to be sure it did not see them before they were ready for it.

HAIR PEACE

"There's a nook in a tree where Worms don't go," Idola said.

"How do you know that?"

"Because their traces are scattered about, but none are there." She focused further. "It—It's the Wormwood Tree."

Wormwood. Something horribly bitter or repulsive. If that repelled the Worms, why not? Idola's Chip clairvoyance was certainly useful. "Take us there."

They stepped off the trail, circling trees, making their way to a particular tree that was a giant among midgets, rising out of the forest into the sky, spreading hugely. It was no pine, but neither was it any other species Quiti could recognize. If her mind was interpreting it, why wasn't it somehow familiar?

"They are not ordinary trees," Flower said, picking up her confusion. "They are special refuges."

"That explains a lot," Quiti said sourly.

The Wormwood Tree's bark was rough but not prickly, providing convenient handholds. Quiti wondered about that, but decided to leave her question for another time, as there was no indication of danger to them. They climbed up the trunk rather than trying to fly, as this used less energy. For all that it wasn't exactly physical energy they used here.

In the center, high above the rest of the forest, was a divergence of great branches forming a kind of platform from which they could view the larger landscape around them. Smaller branches radiated, interlinking, forming a kind of basket or nest. This was the nook, which seemed almost too convenient to be accidental.

Quiti was suspicious. "Why should a tree provide such a handy perch for us, or for anyone?" She had heard of tentacular trees in a fantasy land that lured and consumed unwary creatures. She wasn't sure how that would work with spiritual visitors, but had seen enough of the Worm Web to know that such a threat should not be dismissed casually. "It could be a trap."

"No, they are friendly to us," Flower said. "No Wormwood Tree has ever harmed one of us."

"What do you do for the Wormwoods?"

"I don't know," Flower said nervously.

"Neither do I," Idola said. "Can you read its mind, Quiti?"

Read the mind of a plant? But stranger things had happened on Earth and elsewhere. Quiti focused.

And found the vegetable awareness of the tree. The thing was not only large, it was complicated, with nerves extending throughout the branches and roots. It tracked air, water, soil, distributing resources from and to each as required, and was alert for threats to its security. Its ambiance was tuned to their minds, so it knew they were not hostile to its welfare. That was why it tolerated their presence, when it could have driven them away by projecting a foul odor to their minds. It was not a trap for them, but more like a refuge, just as Flower had said.

But that could not be all. Why should it go to the trouble of assisting passing visitors who were doing it no favors? Since they were here only spiritually, they

HAIR PEACE

neither ate its fruit, whatever it might be, nor excreted potential fertilizer, and had no edible bodies. They did not seem to be assisting it in breeding, either, in the manner of bees with other plants. Yet they had to be offering it something, to cause it to encourage their presence. Nature seldom if ever offered something for nothing.

The question evoked the answer: visitors were sometimes the targets of the Worms. In fact they could lure Worms in. And Worms, being native to the Web, did have sustenance for the tree. Their energy cores were excellent nourishment. Any Worm that entered the tree's close environment was subject to predation.

"We're bait," Quiti announced. "It eats Worms."

Idola clapped her hands. "So this is the perfect place for us, to relax without fear of Worms. It's like Carmen loving carjackers."

"That's nice," Quiti said, amused by the analogy. "But we're not vacationing here. We're just passing through."

"Oh. Yes. But we did stop here to figure out why Flower is afraid of the Worm."

"Oh, yes," Quiti echoed. She turned to the boy. "Why do you fear the Worm? Isn't it just another traveler, as we are?"

Flower burst into tears, his style, flickering wildly and losing coherence.

"I guess not," Idola said, taken aback.

Quiti swept him into her embrace, comforting him in motherly fashion, her hair wrapping around him. Here in the Worm Web he felt perfectly physical, though it was a stick figure she was holding. "I'm sorry, Flower. I thought it was an innocent question."

"I can't answer," he sobbed, more tears dripping from his flower face.

This required finesse. "I just want to understand. May I read your mind?"

"Yes. As long as you hold me close."

She carefully probed his alien mind, starting at the edges and infiltrating cautiously toward the center, all the while holding him in her comforting embrace. A fringe of her own mind marveled at the manner she was separating the physical contact from the mental contact, when they had no physical presence here; it was all interpretation. But since it was working, she did not care to question it.

She got it, much as she had absorbed the information about the tree. Now she spoke to Idola, making it verbal so as not to divert her mental or physical contact with the child: more interpretation.

"Most creatures of the galaxy are planetary, but some are capable of traveling the worm holes when they know how, as we do, spiritually. Some creatures are native to the Worm Web, existing physically, in their manner, in it. The Worms are one such species. Some are borderline, like the Ghobots, native to an original planet but able to travel physically on the Web, because their essence is magnetic, rather than physical. That is how Flower came to us on Earth, physically."

"Wow," Idola said.

"But his species has enemies, and though they escaped to the Worm Web, their enemies hired killers to chase them down and kill them. These are the Worms, who are mercenaries. They don't care about anything themselves, other than survival and energy food, but as hirelings they get a lot of that. They are merciless, not having the wit to appreciate any larger picture. So Flower fears the Worm for good reason. If it catches him, it will kill him."

"How did he escape it before?" Idola asked.

"They knew the Worms had been hired, but the Worms had not yet located the traveling Ghobots. The Worm Web is huge: it's like searching for a dinghy on the Pacific Ocean. The chances of their being found soon were remote."

"But then this Worm—"

"May be random," Quiti said. "Merely cruising around, searching, with no idea its prey was nearby. In which case it should have moved on by now."

"Or—" Idola started grimly.

"Or it got news of our entry to the Web and hightailed from their base over here to intercept us."

"In which case we're in trouble."

"Maybe," Quiti agreed cautiously. "But only if it's that second option. I think it more likely the first option, in which case we can safely resume traveling."

"I don't know," Idola said. "If a Worm tuned in to somebody's entry into the Web, and headed here to check it out, but we skedaddled to the safety of the tree before it quite nailed us, it might play possum to let us think it never saw us, then pounce the moment we come out."

"Smart girl," Quiti said. "I hadn't thought of that."

"Of course I'm smart. I'm a genius now, remember. A Chip off the block. So are you, Hairbrain. You were coming to it next. We need to make a plan that covers all options."

"We do," Quiti agreed. "So let's assume the worst. That the Worm catches us. How do we handle it?"

"Does Flower know?"

Quiti delved back into the child's mind, seeking what he knew of the Worms. "They strike by shooting beams of electro-spiritual shock forward. When it hits a spirit visitor, it blasts it out of the Web and back to the home planet. Harmless in its fashion, but it pretty well disrupts whatever the visitor was doing on the Web. That's the risk we take. When it hits a Web native, it destroys it. That's death. When it hits a borderline individual, like Ghobot, it's like a knockout punch. Then that stunned victim can be taken prisoner, or dumped somewhere out of the action. If it has useful information, it gets interrogated. If it's edible, it gets eaten. If it is sexually appealing, it gets raped. It's not good, regardless." Quiti's imagination balked at the notion of a creature being raped by a worm.

"Is there any defense?"

Quiti checked. "Yes. Mainly avoidance, like hiding or dodging so the shock misses. But a Ghobot who is prepared can bounce it back at the Worm, and if that scores it kills the Worm. Or loop it around and hurl it at someone else. But each defense usually works only once, because while the Worms aren't really smart,

HAIR PEACE

they learn from immediate experience and guard against being balked the same way twice in succession."

"There are three of us, and we can coordinate using your telepathy. Could one of us distract the Worm while the other blasts it?"

"Doubtful. We don't have a weapon against it, except for turning its own weapon against it."

"Suppose I show you exactly where the Worm is, you project an image of Flower for it to fire at, and Flower loops that shot around to hit it in the tail?"

Quiti considered. "Flower, could we do that? Could you catch and redirect the shot if I showed you exactly where it was and where to put it?"

"Right up the Worm's ass," Idola added, laughing.

Flower laughed too. They were after all both children. "Yes," he said.

"Then I think we have a viable combat strategy," Quiti said. "Hoping we don't have to use it." She glanced at Idola. "Are there any other details we should consider?"

"We maybe should try to travel faster than just walking through the woods. So as to cut down our time of exposure."

"Good thought. Walking is simply the way we interpret it. What did you have in mind?"

"A motor scooter?" Idola asked hopefully.

Quiti laughed. "Those things are dangerous. We could get flung off into the lake."

"Then maybe a jet ski, only it jets over land too."

"I could shape it," Flower said, "if you show me how."

"Great!" Idola said, forming a picture in her mind of what vaguely resembled a motorcycle on skis.

Quiti was dubious, but as she considered it, the notion seemed more viable. Which was more dangerous, the vehicle or the delay when deadly creatures were lurking? "See what you can do."

"Do it," Idola told the Ghobot.

Flower formed into the device Idola was picturing. It looked precarious to Quiti. "Enclose it somewhat, to protect us from dust, sleet, branches or stray birds or whatnot."

A shield formed around it. That would have to do. "We'll try it," Quiti said. "But if we get dumped, it's back to walking."

Idola clapped her hands, a mannerism of hers. "We'll zoom!"

Quiti mounted the device, finding the handholds and simple controls. Idola got on behind her, riding shotgun as it were. "Bye, Wormwood!" she called. "Thanks for everything."

They nudged out of the nest and down into the forest, on their way at last.

CHAPTER 6: BEZEL 4

Quiti handled the controls cautiously, getting the feel of them as she slowly guided the craft down to the ground and around the pine trees. Soon she was confident that there were no problems here, as her awareness that this was actually the boy she was rescuing settled into background mode. What a difference the Worm Web made! She emerged onto the original path and picked up speed as they approached the pond. It was true: this was significantly faster than walking.

Of course this was not actually a machine, as she reminded herself again. It was the Ghobot in a robot variation. But here in the Worm Web, reality was what they made it, and this was part of the proof of that. "You okay, Flower?" she inquired.

"I am glad to be of service," his voice came from a grille at the front. She knew he was also glad to have galactics helping him find his way. He could sniff out his own trail himself, but they represented adult reassurance and experience.

They moved out over the pond. Now it was indeed like a jet ski, just touching the surface of the water. Quiti guided it in a circle, enjoying the feel of the ride.

"Uh-oh," Idola said. "It was Option Two."

Now Quiti saw it: a ten foot long shape rather like, yes, a metallic earthworm, tunneling through the air toward them. It had indeed been lurking, waiting for them to depart the safety of the Tree. Now it had them in the open, an easy target. It thought.

Idola's clairvoyance framed the Worm precisely. "Its front cannon is dilating," she reported. "It is about to fire."

Quiti's telepathy put that picture together with the Ghobot's awareness. "Do your thing, Flower," she said.

The Worm fired. The bolt might be traveling at the velocity of light, but in this context they could see it and react to it before it reached them. Again, reality was what they made it, when they had the relevant skills. It came alarmingly close, paused, and was flung back at the Worm.

The Worm exploded in a ball of energy. It was gone.

Idola clapped her hands. "Yea home team! We got it!"

So it seemed, but Quiti remained cautious. This had seemed too easy. "Are there others?"

Idola checked with her mind. "No. This was the only one here."

"So it was a random check," Quiti said. "Entries and exits from the Worm Web must be constant; they had no reason to believe this one was special, so investigated routinely. But there was time to spread the alert: more Worms are bound to be on the way. We had better get out of here."

"Yes. Top speed."

"Which way, Flower?" Quiti asked.

"To our left," the grille replied.

"Uh-oh," Idola said again. "Three more Worms coming toward us from that path."

"They must have picked up Flower's scent trail when he came to Earth," Quiti said. "The same one we are following back. Their search is no longer random."

"Maybe the first Worm alerted them, too," Idola said.

"In which case they have a fair idea that we're armed, in our fashion. We're in trouble. We can't use that trail, and we have to move quickly."

"And find Flower's folks without following his scent trail," Idola said. "That will be a challenge."

Then Quiti got a wicked idea. "They'll be expecting us to flee. So let's surprise them."

"By standing our ground? That should get us wiped out in short order."

"Flower, can you manipulate more than one Worm bolt at a time?" Quiti asked. "If we give your their coordinates and tell you what to do with them?"

"Maybe," he answered uncertainly.

"We'll try it once, then skedaddle. If it works we may be able to use your scent trail after all."

"About to burst onto the pond," Idola said grimly.

"Give them the finger, or whatever insult will enrage them. We want all three to fire simultaneously."

Idola plainly thought this was suicidal, but obeyed. She stood up on the seat, turned around, dropped her skirt and panties, and bent over to expose her bare bottom.

The three Worms burst into sight as Flower giggled appreciatively. Exactly how they perceived Idola's mooning was uncertain, but it worked: all three immediately fired at her.

Meanwhile Quiti was instructing Flower. "Curve the left shot to the right, the right shot to the left," she said, making a mental diagram. "Bounce the center straight back to its source.

As in slow motion, they saw the two side beams make U-turns, while the center one bounced straight back. Three explosions followed.

Idola turned around, drew up her panties and skirt, and viewed the dissipating clouds of smoke. "Wow! I didn't think my bottom would have that effect until I was a big girl."

"It was a good show regardless."

She laughed. "If I'd had more time, I would have farted. That would really have set them off."

What kind of insult to a worm would stomach gas be? But the translation would surely reek. "Now let's follow the trail before more Worms come," Quiti said tersely. "Time is of the essence."

They scooted along the trail, making good progress. But all too soon Idola's clairvoyance picked

HAIR PEACE

up converging Worms. "There must be twenty of them, coming from all sides. We can't handle them."

"We'll have to get off the Web," Quiti said.

"But then we'll lose the trail!" Idola protested.

"We'll recover it later." Quiti scanned the diverging paths for the closest occupied planet.

"Getting close," Idola reported nervously. "All viable Web routes covered. They've got us hemmed in."

"Or so they think," Quiti said. "They don't expect us to jump ship."

The first Worm appeared, orienting on them.

Then Quiti steered for the planet. "Hang on!"

They plunged out of the Web.

They landed in a staging net, where traveling tourist spirits could obtain native hosts for suitable fees. Quiti knew how to bargain that way.

Two alien females transporting a Ghobot child to safe haven. Will trade illicit delights for suitable hosts.

Then two native females put their forelimbs into the net, and Quiti and Idola transferred to their bodies. Flower stayed close, not taking a host: he was not a spirit, but a whole creature.

There was a moment of introduction, telepathically fast, because Quiti and Idola were actually in the minds of their hosts. The hosts were, by Earthly standards, apelike with eye stalks and ear stalks on their heads, and a kind of section trunk for a mouth; but it was easy to make them feel like typical humanoid features. Quiti acquainted her host with her own physical image, then reshaped it to that of a native female. She knew from the native's mind that this was the standard protocol.

Now they spoke with seeming normality, using their hosts' communicatory equipment. "I am Quiti, humanoid female of planet Earth, age 22 in local Earth years, host to a head of Hair. My companion is Idola, age 11, host to a Chip. We are conveying Flower, a lost Ghobot child, back to his family." She returned the trunk to her host. Taking turns was the rule.

"I am Foosha, age 33, native female of Planet Bezel 4. My companion is my sister Geezing, 31. We are hosts only to ourselves."

"We have heard of Hairs, Chips, and Ghobots," Geezing said. "But not encountered any before. This should be interesting."

Then the bargaining for terms. "We want to travel the planet and depart unexpectedly, for we are being pursued by Web Worms we want to lose," Quiti said. "What do you desire?"

"Hot sex," Foosha replied.

"Not feasible, because my companions are children."

"Actually—" Geezing started.

"Not by the rules of our culture," Quiti said firmly.

"If you follow rules, why are you being pursued by Worms?" Foosha asked. "They normally hunt down criminals hiding on the Web."

"We are not criminals. They are after the Ghobot, who is no criminal either, but a child."

"If you say so."

HAIR PEACE

"Read my mind." Quiti opened it to her host.

Foosha was amazed. "You are *that* Quiti! The galactic actress!"

This was an unanticipated complication. "I did not know my fame had spread so widely."

"News of you is in all the Web tabloids. We love your fantasy roles."

"Thank you. But the point was not to brag about my career, but to satisfy you that I am no criminal and that our mission is legitimate."

"We are more than satisfied!"

"Now let's come to terms. We don't feel free to offer erotic pleasures, but what about gustatory?"

"Can you make us taste the banquet you had on Planet J?"

So she really was a fan of their fantasy. "Yes, with Flower's help. You will need to eat something, then we will convert the taste."

"We have plenty of porcine swill bars."

"Those will do. They will taste like Royal Jelly."

They moved on from the staging net, going to a repose site where travelers could rest, snooze, or eat. This was actually a floating sky barge with chambers for rent, more noted for romantic trysts than actual traveling, but questions weren't generally asked. If there was any question about a party of two native females, it was stifled: trysts were not limited to conventional.

Their chamber featured two chairs, a fold-out bed, and privacy shutters. Just so.

Foosha and Geezing took seats and brought out their swill bars, which were the cheapest food available, nourishing but hardly tasty.

Flower, do your thing, Quiti thought.

The Ghobot moved to float invisibly between the two Bezel 4 natives as they bit into their bars, enhancing particular brain waves. There was a pause.

"It is!" Foosha exclaimed, as a look of sheerest rapture infused her face. "It really is!"

"Royal jelly!" Geezing agreed, seeming almost to float.

"Remember, it's just an impression," Quiti reminded them. "Not the real thing."

"That's fine," Foosha said. "Real royal jelly would make us mature into queens."

"And have to be screwed by the drones so as to start popping out eggs continuously," Geezing added.

"The screwing might be fun," Foosha said. "Those drones are really masculine studs."

"But not the continuous egg laying," Geezing said. "It would be like defecating without pause for hours at a time."

"With servitors holding our legs wide open so they could catch every poop."

"Before it cooled."

Then they both laughed. They were clearly well satisfied with the semblance rather than the reality.

I didn't realize there was such a downside to queening, Idola thought.

HAIR PEACE

They're exaggerating, having fun. They're in a gustatory delirium. But it is true that a queen ant or bee is more of a servant than a ruler.

The Bezel women continued their delight, but it soon palled for Quiti and Idola. So Quiti decided to put the time to good use. *Flower*, she thought, including Idola on her telepathic circuit. *Can we dialogue without interrupting the process?*

Yes, if we keep it simple, he responded.

We'll be leaving Planet Bezel 4 when we can do so by surprise. Do you know of ways to foil the Worm pursuit? Things you have seen your folks do in the past?

He pondered briefly. *Yes. There's the scent circle.*

Let me guess, Idola thought. *Like the fox fooling the hounds? I saw that on an ed program.*

An ed program? Quiti thought. *Did a concept get lost?*

ED. Educational, Idola replied. *How nature works. They aren't ALL dull. The hounds are in hot pursuit, but the fox gets a little ahead, then makes a big circle and crosses his own trail, then leaps clear without leaving a scent trace, and the hounds wind up running around and around the circle. They've lost him and don't know it.*

That's it, Flower agreed. *It's supposed to work on dull creatures like Worms.*

Quiti considered. *Your scent trail is what we are following back to your family, and what the Worms are using to intercept you. So a trick like that might work. But I fear only once. We may need more.*

Sometimes we use Em bombs.

Em bomb, Idola thought. *Emotion bomb?*

They discussed it. It turned out that just as they could mark a trail by leaving blazes behind, the Ghobots could detach packets of particular emotions, like joy, fear, grief, anger, or love, which could jerk the applicable brain waves of pursuers and make them unreasonably emotional without warning. This could be real mischief to the unwary. This, too, might work only once or twice, but that might well provide the leeway they needed to escape.

There was a knock on the door. "Oh, poop!" Foosha swore. She raised her voice. "We don't want any! Go away."

"Sorry," a male voice answered. "We two studs saw you two fair damsels board the barge and thought you might want company. We'll leave you alone."

"Men!" Geezing exclaimed.

"Wait!" Foosha called, as the two of them hastily primped. "We thought you were selling something."

"We're just looking for a good time."

"So are we," Geezing said.

"Hold on," Quiti said. "What you do with men is your own business, but I am honor bound to keep the children out of it."

Foosha paused momentarily. "Compromise: we'll split up. You can go with the walking one, while the staying one tackles them both. Then we'll switch. Afterwards, we'll resume the banquet."

Quiti was not completely easy with this, but they did need hosts, so compromise was in order. "We'll do that," she agreed.

HAIR PEACE

The two women opened the door to the two men. "Deal," Foosha said to them. "We have underage company. Choose one of us for the two of you, while the other takes a walk on the deck. After a session we'll switch."

The men exchanged a look, then nodded. This was a bit different, but certainly of interest. "You," the speaker said to Foosha. Quiti's impression was that Foosha was the slightly more attractive one.

Foosha took Geezing's hand, and Quiti hastily joined Idola in Geezing as host, with Flower following outside. Geezing stepped out as the men stepped in. Foosha was already undressing. She was evidently appealing enough, for her age, as the men were not younger.

"I'd rather have stayed and watched," Idola said. "How does one woman do it with two men simultaneously?"

"Never mind!" Quiti snapped.

"We do honor planetary and galactic conventions," Geezing said. "Come, there should be a very nice view." She walked across the deck to the railing at the edge and gazed down. They looked with her, using her eyes.

The barge was floating well above the ground, so that the trees and houses looked small, and the roads resembled twisted threads. Not far above was a passing cloud.

Then it all became impossibly marvelous. They gazed down at the magnificent scene with sheer wonder

Flower! Quiti thought, catching on. *You're enhancing it.*

I thought you'd like it, he thought apologetically.

We do, Idola thought.

Quiti realized that there was no harm in it, and it would distract the children from whatever was happening in the chamber. *We do,* she agreed.

"This is as nice as the food, in its fashion," Geezing said. "What is it?"

"Wonder," Quiti said. "Another emotion, a pleasant one."

"If this is what the Ghobots offer, why are they in bad repute?"

"We suspect it is addiction. Folk get to crave particular emotions too much, and become useless to their societies. So they get banned. But it's only a theory."

"Can they enhance sex similarly?"

"I believe they can."

"Then it's more than a theory."

They circled the deck, chatting, then returned to the chamber. Geezing knocked. Foosha opened the door. She was happily disheveled. "Your turn," she agreed.

They clasped hands, and Quiti and Idola transferred to Foosha. They closed the door and took another walk.

"How does one woman do it with two men at once?" Idola asked as they introduced Foosha to the wonder of the scenery.

"Don't answer that," Quiti said.

HAIR PEACE

Foosha laughed. "Your children are much the same as ours. Always getting into mischief, physical or mental. And no, girl, I will not let you read my mind."

"Poo."

Irritated, Idola extended her clairvoyant awareness. And found something. "Say, there's a little-used wormhole inside that cloud ahead. We might use that and the Worms wouldn't spy us."

"Good idea," Quiti agreed. "We'll take it."

"But your company is just getting interesting," Foosha protested.

Quiti thought fast. "Deal: you let us go quietly so any watching Worms don't know we're gone, and I'll get Flower to make you a sex bomb you can detonate after we're gone."

"Deal!" Foosha agreed. "Those two studs don't know what they're in for!"

"Poo," Idola repeated sullenly.

"Girl, I can give you a partial answer that remains within bounds," Foosha said. "One man kisses her while the other feels her up." That was a very loose translation, for a species that lacked lips or torso ornaments.

"There's got to be more to it than that!"

"Sure. But that part is beyond the limit."

"Flower, make the bomb," Quiti said, not interested in exploring either human or alien limits at the moment. Flower was a child too, but could set up the key brain wave enhancements without experiencing their feelings himself. That would have to do.

Flower got to work on it, and soon had a small magnetic flux. He set it on top of Foosha's head, where it clung statically. It was tuned to the appropriate brain waves, but not yet activating them.

"When you're ready, send a *Detonate!* thought, and the bomb will go off, affecting everyone within its radius," Quiti said. "Make sure you have the men and Geezing close by. It won't last long, but will be intense. You won't be disappointed."

"Thanks!"

"That's a foursome, isn't it?" Idola asked. "Who kisses and feels what?"

"Idola—" Quiti started warningly.

"And *you* can kiss and feel my ass!" But she stopped the questions.

All of which was more show than substance, because the girl could pick up the information clairvoyantly, and probably had. She was pretending ignorance in much the way Quiti was pretending parental-type censorship.

The barge drifted on into the cloud. "Thanks, Foosha," Quiti said. "We are rather different physically and biologically, but maybe not so much culturally."

"Not so much," Foosha agreed. "I will watch your next public show."

"Take my hand," Idola said. Quiti took it, so as to enhance the perception. In a moment she oriented on the wormhole telepathically. It was indeed an old and deserted one that led toward their destination, excellent for their purpose.

"Form the jet ski, as we enter," Quiti told Flower.

HAIR PEACE

"Bye, Foosh!" Idola called as they dived into the wormhole.

CHAPTER 7: WORM CHASE

They were back on the jet ski, moving at speed through an ancient chain of caverns, or so it seemed to Quiti's interpreting mind. There were stalactites hanging from above, and stalagmites rising from below, like closing teeth.

"I can never remember which is which," Idola said.

"There's a mnemonic device," Quiti replied. "The one with the C is for Ceiling, so those hang down. The one with the G is for Ground, so they ascend from below."

"Say, neat!"

Never mind that there could hardly be caves in deep space. It was much less mind bending to see caves than cracks in nothingness.

Then she spied giant bones.

"Dinosaurs!" Idola exclaimed.

Were dinosaurs in space any less credible than caves? Quiti decided not to argue.

"There's my scent," Flower's grill said.

"Okay," Quiti said. "Now we can expect the Worms to be lurking along it, because they know you

HAIR PEACE

have to follow it to find your family. So we had better prepare now, before they intercept us."

"Yes."

"Let's start with the circle. I will loop about, while you lay down the scent."

"Yes."

They emerged from the caves to a mountainous landscape. "There's a mark!" Flower exclaimed.

"I don't see anything," Idola said.

"Only a Ghobot can detect it."

Which was of course the idea. If the Worms could see the marks, they could set up ambushes beside them. "Ignore it for now," Quiti said. "But keep it in mind."

"But if we're following your scent trail—" Idola said.

"Scents are different," Quiti reminded her. "They get left wherever a person goes. We're leaving our own scents. But the marks are deliberate, for jumping to."

Quiti steered around a mountain back to where they had emerged. "Now can you set up a jump to your nearest mark?" Quiti asked Flower.

"Yes."

"But what about us?" Idola asked. "We can't teleport, even in spirit form."

"I am gambling that the Worms are tracking only Ghobots," Quiti said. "So we human spirits are effectively invisible. We're not yet on the enemies list. So we can go wherever we want and they won't notice as long as Flower isn't with us."

"But he *is* with us! That's the whole point of this operation."

"Yes he is. But for this circle trick, we can get away with a brief separation."

"That's pretty nervy."

"We're nervy folk."

Idola smiled, liking that description. "I guess we are."

Flower jumped to his mark, the jet ski disappearing. Then Quiti and Idola walked across to join him. That was all there was to it.

"Now for Part Two," Quiti said. "The back trail."

"The what?"

"The Worms won't know which direction it's going," Quiti explained. "When they follow it one way, they'll wind up on Bezel 4. The other way, the circle. With luck they'll be lost, and by the time they figure it out, we'll be finished and gone."

Idola nodded. "I like it. What now?"

"Now we head for Flower's folks. We come back this way in a hurry when they intercept us." She addressed the Ghobot. "Jump back to the circle. When they are chasing us, and we flee back this way, you jump to your mark and cower down out of sight until they give up in disgust."

Flower jumped back, and they walked back. They boarded the ski jet. Then they diverged from the circle, leaving a new scent trail, seeking his old scent trail.

The scenery changed to a desert with giant cacti. They cruised between them, careful not to touch any.

"Oh, wow!" Idola exclaimed.

HAIR PEACE

"What?"

"A grazing dinosaur."

"Don't be silly. There aren't any living dinosaurs today."

"Oh? Then what is that?" Idola pointed.

"That's a stegosaurus, extinct for maybe seventy million years." Then Quiti paused, eyeing the creature. "But I could be wrong."

"Just a small misplacement in time," Idola said. "What's seventy million years, geologically?"

"Or an interpretation of some alien creature?" Because that was of course the case. Dinosaurs were more familiar than alien monsters.

"Uh-oh."

Quiti was already reading her mind. The Worms had spotted them, or at least Flower. The chase was on. "Flower, reverse course. Go back exactly the way we came, to the circle, and jump and hide. We'll rejoin you in due course."

"But what will I do while I wait? I fidget when I have nothing to do."

"Can't have that," Quiti said seriously. Fidgets might attract attention. "Start making those E-Bombs."

"What kind?"

Quiti kept her patience. He was after all a child. "Make a variety. Each bomb different from the others."

"What if I lose track of which is which? They all look alike from outside."

"That's fine. We want to surprise the Worms."

"Okay." Then, to her relief, Flower shut up.

But Idola didn't. "When they lose us, suppose they make a search pattern? They're bound to find us eventually."

Ouch. "Good point." Quiti thought under pressure. "Flower, the first bomb you make—can you make a Take-No-Notice Bomb? That is, a neutral emotion, an absence of reacting to anything?"

"I think so."

"When they come close to you, don't flee. Detonate that TaNoNo Bomb, the single one you do keep track of, and be perfectly quiet until they pass you by."

"Okay."

"Now scoot." She delivered a mental swat on his nonexistent behind.

The jet ski spun about and zoomed off at top speed. The Worms were in instant pursuit. The fox had been spotted!

Soon they reached the circle. The mountain concealed them for a time, and in that time Flower teleported to his mark. Quiti and Idola, back on foot, simply walked to the side and sat down on a hillock to watch the action.

"I hope you're right," Idola said. "Because if you're not, we're dead meat."

"Remember, if we get blasted here, we'll simply zip right to our bodies back on earth. We're not in real danger regardless."

"Why doesn't it feel that way?"

HAIR PEACE

"Because we're acclimatized to the illusion our spirits have crafted. We tend to believe in it, just as we do in a dream while we're in it. But it's not solid."

"We hope."

"We hope," Quiti echoed, admitting her uncertainty. Theory did not always match reality, devious as this particular reality was.

"I've never been killed before, even in simulation."

"You're not going to get killed this time, either." But there was that lingering doubt.

The posse of Worms burst onto the scene, circling the mountain. Six of them in a pack, like hounds, jostling each other in their eagerness to catch the prey. Each seeming more monstrous than the others. Idola grabbed Quiti's hand.

The posse raced on past them without pausing. They were after all invisible.

The Worms disappeared around the mountain. Quiti and Idola relaxed slightly.

Before long the Worms reappeared, completing the circuit. They rushed on without pausing. They were caught in the loop.

"I'd laugh," Idola whispered. "But they might hear me."

"Probably not, but let's not gamble more than we need to."

After the third circuit, the Worms slowed. They were evidently catching on, maybe smelling their own exhaust fumes.

"We'd better get out of here," Idola said nervously.

"No. Remember, we're part of the scenery."

"But I'm scared!"

"So am I. Sit tight."

The Worms slowed to a halt. Then they evidently received new orders, or reverted to Plan B. They left the scent trail and spread out, canvassing the territory. One came directly toward the two of them. Its gaping disk of a mouth reminded Quiti of a giant blowtorch or laser cannon.

Quiti put her hand on Idola's hand, warning her to stay put. They did not have a NoNo Bomb.

The Worm cruised right by them, so close they could have touched it. It was about a yard in diameter and twenty feet long, floating above the ground. That was larger than the first ones they had encountered, maybe adult rather than teen. Its hide roughly resembled that of a rhinoceros. It had no eyes, ears, or nostrils. Then it was gone, leaving only its own scent trail resembling scorched motor oil. If it had noticed them at all, it was only as incidental wildlife.

Quiti's conjecture had been proved correct. Only Ghobots were on the Worm's radar.

Idola turned to Quiti and hugged her. Then she dissolved into tears. She, too, was a child. Smart, provocative, nervy, but with emotions still being seasoned.

When the coast, figuratively, was clear, they set out to find Flower. Because the Worm search pattern was bound to return to its starting point, and they needed to be gone before that.

HAIR PEACE

"Can you locate him?" Quiti asked Idola, meaning her clairvoyance.

"There doesn't seem to be anything."

That meant his No-Notice Bomb was working.

Quiti ranged out telepathically, focusing, and found his trace of a mind. He was hunkering down, frightened, fearing that they would not come for him.

Flower! Quiti thought. *It's us. We're coming for you.*

Then he was with her too, as frightened as Idola had been. Quiti gave him a mental hug. "You did very well," she said. "The Worms are gone. But we need to get moving before they return."

The NoNo field faded, done in by their discovery of Flower. He transformed to the jet ski and they resumed motion.

"Sniff out your original scent trail again," Quiti said. "But keep your Bombs ready, because the Worms are bound to intercept us once more before we get far, and this time they will be wary of a loop."

Flower did, and soon they were scooting at speed along the trail.

Sure enough, they careened into another nest of Worms. "Flee in any direction," Quiti directed. "But wiggle it, so there's no straight line for them to follow. Curve generally around so as to intercept the trail farther along."

The jet ski did. But this time the Worms did not let them get out of sight. Soon they were closing in from behind, the lead one almost close enough to fire a shot.

"Nobody loves me, everybody hates me," Idola sang. "Think I'll go eat worms." A nice inversion, considering that it was far more likely that the Worms would eat *them*. The girl was irrepressible. Chances were that she would one day be Quiti's daughter in law. That was not a bad prospect.

"Drop a Bomb," Quiti said tersely to Flower. "Any Bomb."

There was a slight pop as something shot out of the ski's rear. "He dropped a turd on them!" Idola said, tittering.

In a moment the first Worm smacked into the invisible Bomb and reacted. It sailed up high, performing an odd undulation.

"What's it doing?" Idola asked, perplexed.

Quiti read the creature's limited mind. "It's dancing for joy," she reported. "That was a Joy Bomb."

"And you know, it's not chasing us anymore," Idola said. "It's too busy basking in its own ecstasy."

"So a positive emotion can be as effective a deterrent as a negative one," Quiti agreed, impressed.

But the next Worm, not struck by the Bomb, was already closing in on them, its circular maw dilating for a blast. "Loose another," Quiti said. They did not want to get struck by a shot.

"Yeah, poop on them again," Idola agreed.

There was another faint rear pop. Then the second Worm, so close it must have swallowed the Bomb whole, reacted.

HAIR PEACE

It slowed while still orienting on them. It seemed to be studying them intently with its eyeless face, making no aggressive move.

"What's it feeling?" Idola asked.

Quiti checked. "Wonder."

"Like us gazing at the clouds on Bezel 4? Wow!"

Quiti smiled. "I suppose our jet ski could be pretty impressive, considered that way."

"Maybe it's the taste of the poop. Worms like poop, don't they?" Idola was barely suppressing her avalanche of stifled giggles.

But now the third Worm was advancing, nosing the second to the side.

"Next Turd, I mean Bomb," Quiti said. There was a pop.

The third Worm wriggled in place, then dropped back to float parallel to the fourth Worm. Marksmanship was easy, since they were all on the same scent trail.

"Are they ganging up on us?" Idola asked.

Quiti did not take the chance, despite not yet knowing the nature of the Bomb. "Next."

The fourth Bomb caught the fourth Worm. For a moment it froze in place.

Worm Three suddenly curled around Worm Four.

"Sex!" Quiti said, finally reading its mind. "It wants to make love."

"And there's a child watching," Idola chortled. "Have they no shame?"

Worm Four's tail whipped about, smacking Worm Three amidships. It was no incidental blow; a chunk of hide flaked off.

"And Four just got a dose of Rage," Quiti said.

"Hoo boy! This should be fun!"

Three was determined, as such an emotion took little note of pain. But Four, enraged, was in no mood to accommodate. She turned her snout and blasted Three with a snootful of laser. It almost burned his head off, but still his body wrapped around hers seeking romantic access. Quiti was reminded of the way praying mantises made love, with her biting his head off while he continued mating undeterred.

"Wow," Idola breathed. "Violent porn."

The two Worms twisted off the path, drifting aside in the course of their struggle. The following Worms, confused by the actions of the first four, drifted back uncertainly.

"I'd say we have an adequate defense," Quiti said, allowing a smile to escape.

"Make Love *and* War," Idola agreed zestfully.

But still more Worms were pressing forward. "Another," Quiti said grimly.

"This is almost fun."

The next Worm got hit. It abruptly turned tail, literally, and fled. "That was Fear," Quiti said with satisfaction.

It was not enough. The Worms were either catching on that there was only one Bomb at a time, or becoming so eager for the kill that they were crowding

HAIR PEACE

up closely regardless. This was a losing ploy, in the long run.

"Damn," Quiti said. "I don't think we can make it, on this go-round. I think we'll have to retreat to Earth, plan our mission, and try again, better prepared. I'm sorry, Flower."

"I see the Worms," the speaker grille said. He did understand the situation.

"Very well. Loose all your remaining Bombs, and we'll hightail it out of here in the ensuring confusion."

There was a series of pops. Then the poop hit the fan, as it were. Suddenly the Worms were reacting in multiple ways, causing chaos.

Quiti called out as many as she could, while she steered the jet ski in the direction she knew: toward Earth. "Happiness, sorrow, hope, frustration, disappointment, gratitude, embarrassment, pride, shame, remorse, longing, love, hatred, worry, relief, jealousy, humiliation, insecurity, resentment, betrayal, dread, desperation, resignation, despair. More I can't sort out at the moment."

"Reverence, disgust, gluttony," Idola added, identifying some by their external manifestations. "What a scene!" Because the Worms were now in a spaghetti like mass of struggling creatures, trying to handle emotions they seldom if ever experienced in their normal lives.

But a few were on the outside, having avoided the Bombs, and these were orienting for another charge. There were no Bombs left. It was definitely time to depart.

Quiti zeroed in on the wormhole she needed. "Hang on!" she called as she guided the jet ski there.

They plunged into the hole, and through it, to emerge back on Earth. There was a moment of disorientation.

Quiti stirred. She was back in her material body. She looked across at Idola, whose eyes were blinking. And at the flickering stick figure that was Flower. They had made it safely home.

"It's good to have you back," Gena said as she went to tend to her daughter. "We have I think a nice surprise for you."

"A surprise?" Quiti asked blankly.

"She arrived a few minutes ago, following Flower's scent trail. We have been conversing in the interim."

"She?"

"I call her Orchid, as her real name has no feasible translation."

Mommy! Flower exclaimed mentally.

Mommy?

Then Quiti saw the blurry figure embracing Flower, and read the attendant mind. It was indeed his Ghobot mother. Who had naturally been looking for her lost child, just as he was looking for her. All they had really had to do was wait.

CHAPTER 8: TRIO

"She's some woman," Gena confided to Quiti. "I believe the Ghobots can have a place here on Earth, if we can work out the details."

Quiti looked at her with surprise. "Are you changing sides?"

Gena laughed. "I was never on a side, Quiti. I merely questioned whether it would be smart to have the Ghobots here on Earth, given their history."

"And now you don't?"

"I still do question it. But my brief dialogue with Orchid satisfies me that this could use more exploration."

"You like her."

"I certainly do. But there's bound to be more to it than that."

Quiti was pleased. Gena was the most sensible member of the Embassy, and her acquisition of both Hair and Chip powers only amplified that. If she thought there was a prospect, it was an excellent signal.

The larger Ghobot separated from the smaller one and faced them, in a manner. *I wish to thank you, Quiti and Idola, for taking care of my son.*

"Pause," Gena said. "We appreciate that Ghobots do not speak verbally, but since we humans do, and we have a telepathic environment here, let's automatically translate Orchid's thoughts to be received as verbal. We know that others won't hear her speak, if they're aware of her at all, but we are the ones who matter in this circumstance."

"Thank you," Orchid said.

Just like that!

"Flower helped a lot," Idola said. "We loved those E-Bombs."

"E-Bombs?"

"Emotion Bombs," Quiti said, sending her a descriptive thought. "They stopped the Worms from catching us."

"Ah."

"Idola, why don't you take Flower out and show him the neighborhood?" Gena suggested. "There is a significant chance that he will remain on Earth, so it may help him to better understand it."

"Oh, poo! You're banishing the children from the hot sex talk."

"Of course, dear. Nominally protecting your fraying innocence. You won't be servicing any pedophiles."

Idola grumbled, but obeyed. "Come on, Flower. We can maybe toss some Disgust Bombs at passing matriarchs."

"Idola—"

The girl laughed. "Maybe not today. We want to lie low." She had been teasing her mother back.

The two of them departed.

"What is on your mind?" Quiti asked.

HAIR PEACE

"If we are to invite the Ghobot clan to come to Earth," Gena said, "we need to be sure there is suitable work for them that won't stir controversy. Orchid is unfamiliar with the nuances of our global culture, so I thought I'd bounce them off you."

"But I'm not objective. I want to help them."

"To be sure. But you will be aware of the pitfalls."

"Go on."

"I am thinking of the things that Ghobots can do that we can't. Such as yes, Emotional Enhancement. Also spot Teleportation. And slight Precognition. There could be a potent market for such things here."

"A dangerous one," Quiti said.

"Exactly. I don't think we can afford to advertise them."

"Then how can we use them? Word will get out the first time they are used in public."

"Yes. The key may be to conceal their use."

"You have any idea how to do that? There's no concealing the effect of a Sex Bomb once it detonates."

"Ah, but there may be. An impotent man with an appealing woman in a conducive environment may attribute his surprising success to that environment."

"And think she's faking it," Quiti agreed. "Or that she's carried away by his sheer masculinity. Men like to think that."

"Yes. Men can be manageable. As for the others, Precognition can be taken as a lucky guess. But Teleportation is a challenge, unless done unobserved."

"So there may be ways to conceal the use of Ghobot powers," Quiti said. "Where is this leading?"

"It seems possible that on other planets, the full potentials of the Ghobots were not at first appreciated. But when they became apparent, and public hunger for them went on a rampage, the danger made the visitors unwelcome."

Quiti looked at Orchid. "Is that what happened?"

"To a degree," the woman said. "We tried our best to conceal them, but the necessity to earn our living required us to use our abilities more than was in retrospect wise."

"Like hunger forcing theft of a loaf of bread," Quiti agreed.

"I do not understand."

That was right: Ghobots did not eat. "Bread provides sustenance," Gena explained. "It is food. Without food, we suffer and die."

"Oh, yes. We have seen that elsewhere. I was thinking of the hunger for status, love, or sex."

"Which doesn't come in loaves," Quiti said. "But if you don't need to eat, and I think you don't need housing or clothing, what is it you have to trade for?"

"Status. We want to be recognized as an independent species worthy of respect."

"But it seems humans aren't the only species that likes to push down a minority," Gena said.

Quiti thought of the Gypsies and the Jews and other minorities. "So how can it be different here?"

"That's what I'm working on," Gena said. "Suppose we addressed prisoner reform?"

Quiti was startled. "What could that have to do with this? We don't want the Ghobots to be prisoners."

HAIR PEACE

"Prisoners don't have much freedom. They have to take what they can get. Suppose they could get an hour with a homely courtesan and a covert Sex Bomb if they behaved?"

"They'd behave for a day or so," Quiti agreed. "She wouldn't seem homely when the Bomb went off."

"It could be a daily routine. A special conducive chamber."

"You would soon have a model prisoner."

"They have done that elsewhere," Orchid said. "Soon the guards would cheat the prisoners out of their hours, so the guards could experience the chamber. There were riots."

Quiti nodded. "For which the Ghobots got blamed, of course."

"So the viability of prison reform is limited," Gena said. "Because of the inherent corruptibility of sapient species."

"But you have something in mind."

"This may be a stretch, but I'm considering mass killers."

Quiti shook her head. "I think you're losing me."

"I am thinking of using the Ghobot precognition to anticipate such crimes, perhaps by reading the future headlines, and then to go to prevent them happening."

"Isn't that paradox? Once it happens, it happens."

"I think there is no paradox if it's a future crime. This is merely a better way to anticipate it and stop it."

"Like that movie, *Minority Report*? I think they had problems anyway."

"Carefully and anonymously done, problems might be bypassed."

"I'm not sure," Quiti said. "We're messing with reality. One mistake and it might be impossible to recover."

"That's why I think we should rehearse it first. Before saying anything about it to anyone else."

"That's why you banished the children! Because they'd be bound to blab."

"Better to let then think we are talking about sex," Gena agreed.

"So how do we rehearse it?"

"First I believe we should form a team of three: you, me, and Orchid. We need to get to know and trust each other so we can be fully coordinated. Then we can integrate our relevant talents: clairvoyance, telepathy, precognition. We can identify some local crime—it doesn't have to be a mass killing, just something that needs to be prevented—and arrange to prevent it. If we fail, it's minor anyway. If we succeed, we can go on to something larger. In an easy stage."

Quiti remained wary, but it did seem to make sense. Preventing mass killings was certainly worthy, and if the Ghobots made it possible, their welcome on Earth seemed guaranteed.

The two human women spread their telepathy, taking Orchid in. More rapidly than could ever be feasible with spoken or written dialogue, they got to know each other well. It was considerably more intimate than sex, because the truest privacy was being yielded: that of the mind. Gena was right: Orchid was a

HAIR PEACE

very fine woman, one Quiti would like to have for a lifelong friend. She had solid experience in romance, having met and married her husband and borne (not birthed) their child. She had a number of skills, such as playing the magnetic harp, a musical instrument that did not exist on Earth, and doing the equivalent of card tricks. In fact she could spot a card cheat almost before he started. She could dance, Ghobot style, which might not mean much to a human audience but was phenomenally sexy to a Ghobot.

And she could precog. This was most accurate close up, such as telling whether an about to be flipped coin would land heads or tails. Quiti flipped a coin numerous times, in and out of Orchid's sight, and the woman never missed. In fact she even knew when Quiti was about to try a ruse, such as balking at the last moment. But each minute ahead made it more chancy, as it were. At five minutes the odds were still two to one, but beyond that there was little point.

But coin flips were minor. The woman could tell them when their Embassy phone was about to ring, and listed four calls in the next fifteen minutes, all of which came to pass. She could call out what the Food of the Day would be at the Embassy. And she spotted the appearance of a crazed man one day hence who would seek to sneak into the embassy so he could try to rape Quiti.

"Now there's a good test case," Gena said, smiling. "That kook doesn't have a chance, of course: Quiti would spot him telepathically long before he got close. The embassy security guard would arrest him before he ever got in. If he actually caught her, she would overpower him bare handed because of her Hair Power strength. Or she could even let him penetrate her, and clamp off his member and pull it right out of his body by its root. Raping a Hair or Chip is an idiotic dream. But let's see if we can defuse this with no incident at all. How should we do it?"

"Give the guard the afternoon off," Quiti said. "And give me a Fear Bomb."

"Why not. That would test the case readily enough." Gena smiled. "But now let's see if there's anything more serious we can tackle."

They showed Orchid a typical newspaper page on the screen. "This shows what has happened recently," Quiti explained. "Mostly incidental and routine. Can you see tomorrow's edition, or even the modified evening edition?" She made the basic nature of the paper clear mentally, as it was foreign to the Ghobot's experience.

Orchid focused, and in a moment saw the afternoon edition. They read it in her mind. There were three new headlines, and some deleted stories. Quiti made careful note of the contents. Then Orchid moved on to the midnight edition. One item was fuzzy, evidently subject to change, but the others were firm. Quiti noted these too. Finally they tried for the tomorrow morning edition—and scored.

There was a mass shooting. It was a small one, only three dead and six injured, and it was a thousand miles away, but it was what they sought. It was

HAIR PEACE

tomorrow's paper, but the incident was tonight, two hours away.

"Damn!" Quiti said. "I'd like to try for this one, not waiting for the rapist."

They discussed it and decided to try. Gena sent her daughter a mental message to return to the Embassy and babysit it with Flower. Then the three of them oriented on a local wormhole crevice, with Quiti exploring it mentally and tracing the several bypaths, selecting the route they wanted. Quiti and Gena lay back in their easy chairs, while Orchid oriented on Gena's mind so she could follow her physically.

They plunged into the crevice, and instantly were in the other city, a back alley where the crevice happened to emerge. They walked toward the site of the coming massacre. Gena extended her clairvoyance and Quiti her telepathy, and surveyed the area.

And found the mind of the killer. He was collecting his weapons hardly a block away, intending to walk to an overpass and blast away at anyone in the vicinity. At exactly ten PM he would do it. It was important that the time be just right. Quiti wasn't sure exactly why, but didn't care; she just wanted to see if they could foil the crime.

"Uh-oh," Gena said. "We can't get there from here. There's a foot patrolman who will intercept us, not the killer." Orchid's precog verified that: it was destined to happen, if they let it.

Quiti looked at her watch. "We have fifteen minutes."

They considered, then hurried around the block, avoiding the patrolman. While they walked, Quiti explored further, seeking the motive. It turned out that he was furious because his girlfriend had walked out on him, just because he stole some of her money. He couldn't hurt her because he loved her, but he had to hurt *someone*. So he would kill anyone who walked past her house at ten, when she was changing for bed and might be glimpsed through the not quite shuttered window, and that would expiate it. Quiti did not quite follow the logic, but realized that he was not completely rational. His reasoning was good enough for *him*, and that was what counted.

"So what do we do with him?" Gena inquired. "We don't want to get into killing anyone; the point is to stop that kind of thing. But if we don't deal with him, he will kill someone else, now or another time."

Quiti had an idea. "Orchid, can you make an Amnesia Bomb? I know that's not exactly an emotion."

"Yes. It is the absence of emotion, and can be done."

"Good. Make me one to use on the killer. I want him to forget what made him mad, and to forget what he was planning to do about it. Maybe even forget that he had had a girlfriend. That way nobody gets hurt."

Orchid made the Bomb. Quiti took it and set it in a pocket. It was nothing but a small magnetic flux, giving no hint of its real nature.

They got there at seven minutes to ten—but under the overpass, not on it. Damn!

"He is on his way," Gena said.

HAIR PEACE

Quiti searched desperately. There was no convenient entry to the overpass right here. It would take too long to go to the nearest access, and the killer would be sure to see them.

"Orchid, do you foresee a way?" Quiti asked desperately.

"It is complicated. There are many options, but they are unfamiliar to me. I need time to sort them."

Just so. Meanwhile the man was arriving on the overpass. He was right on time, of course walking to it at five minutes before ten. "He is lifting his rifle off his shoulder," Gena reported.

Quiti acted without thinking. "Take that!" she said, and hurled the Bomb up at him. She might not be a great baseball player, but she did know how to throw things.

There was a soundless flash as it struck.

"Time to get out of here," Gena said urgently. "That patrolman is coming."

They took a worm crevice back home.

"Now the news," Quiti told Orchid. "Can you find that same edition?"

In a moment the Ghobot had it. There was no headline of a killing; that news had disappeared.

"I think we did it," Gena said. "Despite complications. But there is certainly food for thought. We need to plan the next mission better."

"Scouting for overpasses and patrolmen," Quiti agreed.

But overall they were well satisfied. They told the children what they had done, and the complications.

"Piss happens," Idola said. They found a private nook for Orchid and Flower and turned in.

In the morning, Quiti checked the regular edition of the newspaper, not the foretold one. It was the same as what they had seen, without that headline, but now she had time to check the back pages, looking for anything relating to that particular city at that time.

"I found something," she said.

Gena was on it. "Oh?"

"They found this man wandering around, confused. He was of interest because of his guns. He seemed to have partial amnesia. He said he had this vague notion there was to be a killing there. He concluded that maybe he had gone there to *foil* a killing, and might have scared away the killer. It seems he is a minor hero, at least for the moment."

Gena laughed. "Piss happens," she said, echoing her daughter. "But now it's definite: we need to plan more carefully. I think we'd better get some more experience before we start training crews."

"Crews?"

"One Hair, one Chip, one Ghobot. Invaluable for preventing crimes."

"So you have concluded that the Ghobots can come here?"

"Why not. With one trifling little detail: how do we keep the corruption out?"

"I will work on that," Quiti said.

"We all will work on that," Gena said. "I have an intuition that this is important. Very important."

HAIR PEACE

"I do too," Quiti said. "Logically, yes, of course it is important. It could save innumerable lives. But there is something else."

"I do, also," Orchid said. 'I have looked into the near future many times, for incidental things like avoiding unpleasant encounters or seeking pleasant ones. But this is so much more than that. When I connect with the two of you, becoming part of the Trio, I feel a rare empathy and power I have not experienced before. You are good people, I am sure, but that is not the point of this. I sense that we are on the verge of a truly remarkable discovery."

"Something vastly more important than stopping future mass killings," Quiti said. "Yet that makes me wonder, because what could such a thing possibly be?"

"I wonder too," Gena said. "Yet I feel that it is so."

The three women gazed at each other, physically and mentally, marveling.

"Let's take a break to powder our noses or whatever," Gena said. "Then return to tackle this whatever it is. Because my intuition suggests that it is not only big, but urgent."

"Like anticipating motherhood," Quiti said. "Are we on the verge of changing our lives more significantly than we can comprehend at this moment?"

"It is frightening, yet wonderful," Orchid agreed.

They took their break, knowing that their lives might never again be this incidental.

CHAPTER 9: WONDER WORM

"You're in charge, Idola," Gena said. "You and Flower do whatever you want to, but stay out of mischief, and cover for us. We don't know how long we'll be out. With luck, under an hour."

Idola nodded, understanding. She was a perky, sassy, independent girl, but she had caught on that something serious was forming, and knew better than to interfere. The three would be right there in the room with her, physically, but absent mentally. They weren't even going into the wormholes this time, just into the Trio.

Quiti and Gena moved their chairs to be side by side, and settled into them, holding hands for closest interaction. Orchid curled around those linked hands, her magnetism infusing them. They were as close as they could be to one, physically. The three of them merged, mentally.

A scene formed around them, a pleasant glade within a forest, with the hint of rabbits and sparrows in the background.

HAIR PEACE

"Now what are we here for?" Quiti asked. She was thinking rather than physically speaking, but the convenience of the emulation was what counted. It was a rhetorical question. None of them knew exactly what they sought, but all of them knew it was overwhelming.

"Maybe Eternity," Gena replied.

"I do have a notion," Orchid said. "We seek the Future. For the news events."

"We do," Quiti agreed. "But I think that is only the beginning."

"Let's manifest visually as well as sonically," Gena said. "For comfort, so that we can better focus on the mission." She formed an image of herself as a handsome woman in her thirties, garbed in a comfortable robe that did not conceal her shapeliness. She was standing at the edge of the glade.

Quiti followed suit, appearing with her hair now showing as hair rather than clothing. It clung to her body, outlining her curves. It was her hair that defined her, and she was glad to show it off. She stood beside her friend.

Orchid manifested as a dark and pretty Gypsy woman, similarly shapely, as this was the human translation of how she appeared to others of her own kind. She stood on the other side of Gena. There was also a certain quality about her, like a lovely bloom, as befitted her name.

They were all attractive females, and proud of it. Any of them could fascinate a male of their own kind with ease, and did not mind doing it as often as the mood struck. Their males really appreciated that.

"Now, what do we each bring to this engagement?" Gena asked. "When I became both Hair and Chip, I discovered that I could dream the future with close enough accuracy to use it." She smiled. "That is how I got my husband. I dreamed I seduced him, then went and did it physically. He never had a chance."

"He never wanted a chance," Quiti said. "Any more than mine did."

"Or mine," Orchid said. "Seduction of eager males is the easiest art."

"Now it occurs to me that my ability is a kind of precognition," Gena said. "That may overlap your precognition, Orchid."

"It may," the Ghobot agreed. "Two species of a type."

"I have no precognition," Quiti said. "But my telepathy lets me borrow yours."

"Your telepathy is a marvelous asset," Orchid agreed. "It is what unifies us mentally. I think with that, and Gena's clairvoyance, we can forge a stronger sense of the future."

"I'm not sure that the future is precisely what we seek," Gena said. "For our immediate mission, yes, but I suspect there is something beyond that. Is there a larger framework?"

"There is," Orchid said. "The future as we see it is merely an aspect of the space-time complex. I have on occasion glanced into the near past. It is all part of the larger continuum."

HAIR PEACE

"How will the past help us with our mission?" Quiti asked.

"Often the past clarifies the future," Gena said. "We better appreciate the significance of what we see in the future if we understand its origin in the past."

"And if we grasp the mindset of those who participate in it," Orchid said.

Quiti nodded. "Now I can appreciate that. A general appreciation of the things and people of the world should help us see the future they make. Shall we now try for tomorrow's newspaper headlines?"

"We've done that," Gena said. "Let's try for next week's headlines."

"Or next month's," Orchid said.

Quiti was surprised. "That far?"

"Indeed. Distance is not our problem; accuracy is."

"Accuracy," Quiti repeated, thoughtfully. "It occurs to me that maybe we don't have to depend on a secondhand source, like a newspaper. At least not entirely. Could we peek at the future more directly?"

"How do you mean?" Gena asked.

Quiti hesitated. "I'm not quite sure, but there's something."

"I know what she means," Orchid said. "To visit a host in the future, so as to pick up the full sensual and emotional range of the event."

"Yes, that's it!" Quiti agreed. "The host can read the headlines."

"Interesting," Gena said. "Perhaps we can select hosts, and orient on them. But who?"

Quiti drew a blank, but again Orchid, more experienced than she in this respect, drew it from her mind. "Ola for Quiti, Pacifa for Gena."

"Who?" Gena asked.

"The lesbian couple!" Quiti exclaimed, sending a mental description. "I danced with Ola."

"And Pacifa is like me," Gena agreed, picking up on it. "Except for sexual orientation. I like her."

"That's two," Quiti said. "What of you, Orchid?"

"I am sharing the two of you as my Trio hosts. I don't need another."

"One thing," Gena said. "Will they be aware of us?"

"Yes, if you make yourselves known," Orchid said. "It will be like planetary hosts, only from a different time rather than a different planet."

"Foosha and Geezing," Quiti said, sending information about the two Bezel 4 women. "I was in Foosha."

"And my daughter was in Geezing," Gena said, assimilating it.

"A similar association," Orchid agreed.

"Then let's do it," Quiti said. "I will orient on Foo—I mean Ola, one month hence."

"And I on Pacifa," Gena agreed. "If I can figure out how to do it."

"No need," Orchid said. "I know how. But I am sensing something else. Something monstrous, just beyond one month, here."

"Me too," Quiti said.

"So do we avoid it, or go for it?" Gena asked.

HAIR PEACE

"Go for it," Quiti said. "It could be a record killing."

Orchid nodded. "To the monstrous, the time and place. Yield to my imperative."

They yielded, and suddenly Quiti was in Ola.

Hello Ola, she thought. *May I visit with you?*

The girl was startled. "Quiti! Why am I suddenly thinking of you?"

Because I am visiting you spiritually from your past. My friend is visiting your friend. We are on an important mission. May we stay long enough to accomplish it?

Ola looked across at Pacifa, who was washing dishes. "Yes," Pacifa said. "Either my imagination is running riot, or I am being visited from the past by a member of the Hair Suit Embassy staff named Gena. She's quite a gal."

"So is Quiti," Ola said. "She's the one who got us together."

"I know, and I thank her daily for that. I love you, Ola."

"And I love you, Pacifa. But I gather they are not here to experience lesbian love."

"They are not," Pacifa agreed, amused.

"This may not be nice," Quiti said through Ola's voice. "There is something huge and awful about to happen. We need to learn what it is, so that we can return to our own time and try to prevent it."

"Such as what?" Ola asked, taking back her voice.

"Such as a big mass killing," Gena said through Pacifa's voice. "Or a devastating explosion."

"We certainly want to help stop that," Ola said.

There was a rumble from outside.

"Or maybe an earthquake," Quiti said.

"But this is not an earthquake zone," Pacifa said.

They went to the window and looked out. "Oh, no!" Quiti said, appalled. A building across the street was collapsing, but that was only part of it.

"What is that?" Ola asked, amazed.

"It's a wormhole Worm," Quiti said. "A deadly creature. I thought they couldn't exit to a planet."

They can exit, just as Ghobots do. When so directed.

"That thought," Pacifa said. "That's not either of you."

"That's Orchid Ghobot," Quiti explained, sending a clarifying thought. "A galactic traveler who has encountered the Worms before. She is with us."

"Who sent the Worm here?" Ola asked. "And why?"

Whoever sent the Worms after my son, Orchid thought. *That's the horrendous event: the Worms are attacking your home turf.*

The Worm fired another blast, and the rest of the building collapsed into smoking rubble. It wriggled on past.

"Where is it going?" Ola asked, horrified.

"South," Pacifa said.

Suddenly Quiti understood. "City Hall. The Hair Suit Embassy. It's gunning for *us*."

"But why?" Gena asked.

HAIR PEACE

Because you have taken in the Ghobots, Orchid thought. "By the time of this future."

Quiti realized it must be true. "But have they ever done that before? I mean, gone after you on a planet?"

Not that we know of. This does seem extreme.

There was another sound. They left the house so as to look for it.

There was another Worm blasting through buildings a few blocks to the west. And a third to the east.

"It's an invasion," Gena said.

"But if they're after the embassy, why not just go there directly and blast it?" Quiti asked.

"You know the answer to that," Gena said wryly. "The wormholes don't always go where you want to go."

Quiti remembered how they had had to detour and go part of the way to the killer on foot. The Worm army must have needed a very large hole, and the closest one must have been several miles away from the Embassy. So now they were systematically blasting their way toward it, heedless of the collateral damage, if they even noticed it.

"We've got to stop them!" But Quiti couldn't think how. This was not a matter of avoiding the Worms, but of stopping them short of their target, quite another matter.

You forget; you don't stop them physically. You stop them by removing the target before they strike.

"Those are my friends out there!" Ola cried, wresting control of her body from Quiti and running toward the closest Worm as it oriented on another house. "Shoo! Shoo go away!"

"Ola!" Pacifa said. "Stay away from it!"

Too late. The Worm evidently heard her. Its snout whipped about and a jet of energy shot out. It caught the girl squarely, incinerating her.

Quiti woke in her own body in the Embassy, transfixed by horror not for herself but for Ola, who had foolishly sacrificed her life.

Then Gena returned, and Orchid.

"I told Pacifa we'd unhappen it," Gena said. "Because we have a month to do so. If we can't stop the Worm raid, we can at least go back to an interim time and warn them. Ola won't die."

"Thank you," Quiti said. Then she dissolved into tears. This experiment had abruptly become savagely personal.

Later they discussed it in more detail. "Someone will send the Worms to wipe us out," Gena said. "I don't think it can be just because we sheltered a Ghobot or two. The Ghobots simply aren't that important on a galactic scale. There has to be another reason."

"I agree," Orchid said. "We have been persecuted before, but never in this manner. Something else is occurring."

"But what else could it be?" Quiti asked. "The only thing that has changed recently is the arrival of two Ghobots."

"This is true," Orchid said. "But there may be another aspect. That is the Trio. The three of us have

HAIR PEACE

combined to discover a way to explore the future in greater distance and detail than before. That is potentially quite significant."

"It is," Gena agreed thoughtfully. "Our recent excursion will enable us to foil the Worm invasion, or at least save some lives, because now we know when and where it will come."

"It may be more than that," Orchid said. "We may be developing a mental technology of discovery that could change the future enormously. If there are entities already using such techniques, they may be hostile to such development in other minds."

"Like Earth's nuclear powers being hostile to new nuclear powers on Earth, Quiti said. "They might well strike preemptively before those new powers developed enough to do it back to them."

"They might indeed," Gena said. "That does make sense. But the big question remains: Who?"

"I do not know," Orchid said. "But it occurs to me that you, Gena, are unique in one manner: you are the only creature extant who possesses three cultures."

"Question?"

"You are Human. Also Hair. Also Chip. That is three. I have not known of anyone in the galaxy with three, though of course my knowledge is not complete."

Gena shrugged. "The combination does seem to have given me my future dreaming ability. Regular Humans, Hairs, or Chips can't do it, so it must be a frisson, an effect of overlapping."

"Or an emergent quality," Orchid said. "It is possible that dreams are only the beginning of your ability."

"I suppose. But I have no idea what else there might be."

"Let's assume for the moment that there is more. And that when you merge with Quiti and with me, there is more yet. That this is something like your world's nuclear power. Something potentially quite dangerous to others. That might cause some other power to make a preemptive strike to eliminate it."

Quiti saw it. "Before it becomes complete, because after that it's too late."

"Exactly," Orchid said.

"But that would mean that we are not merely trying to prevent the Worm strike," Gena said, "but that we are actually the cause of it."

The three of them gazed at each other with an expanding surmise. Could their innocent melding have galactic ramifications? That was awesome—and scary.

"I think we had better figure this out right now," Quiti said. "Our lives may depend on it."

"They may indeed," Orchid agreed. "That future Worm strike is our warning. We have the advantage of knowing it is coming. This is our avenue of opportunity to save ourselves and possibly our several species."

"I agree," Gena said. "But *how?*"

"Dream."

"But we've already done the dream of the Worm invasion. I think the best we can do is to warn others of it, if they'll listen."

HAIR PEACE

"No," Quiti said. "This may be like the genie who grants the peon one wish. The dull one wishes for fame, fortune, or the perfect romantic partner. The smart one wishes for a hundred more wishes."

"That loophole was closed after the first telling of the story," Gena said. "You can't chop up a wish without ruining it."

"Figurative," Quiti said. "My point is that we need to find a truly superior wish, such as for universal enlightenment. Or in this case, a more informative dream."

"A dream of enlightenment," Gena agreed. "That does make sense."

"But with us included," Orchid said. "We all need enlightenment."

"Then let's do it." Gena settled into her chair and extended her hand, and Quiti took it as she settled into her own chair. Orchid wrapped around their link.

Soon they were back in the timeless glade, which seemed to be their joint home base. They were the three appealing women. "This time we are not seeking the future," Orchid said. "We seek enlightenment."

"Are we looking for other hosts?" Quiti asked.

"I think not," Gena said. "Hosts may be too limiting to some particular place or time. We need to be free to range anywhere."

"As long as we do it together," Orchid said.

"But just asking for enlightenment doesn't seem specific enough," Quiti said. "We need to orient on something more tangible."

"The source," Gena said. "The root cause of our problem. Understand that, and we may be on the way to discovering what we need."

"The source," Orchid agreed. "Clear our minds, except for that. Then go into our discovery state."

They did. Then they were flying, the three of them like misty sylphs, up out of the glade, the forest, into the upper atmosphere and on into space beyond the planet. Then into deep space, beyond the sun, and beyond the galaxy. They were going somewhere, with no notion where or when. They weren't using the existing wormhole crevices, but floating along beside them. It was as if they were fashioning their own crevices, in the dream.

They came to a fractured planet where the crevices of the wormholes overlapped those of the globe's core. There tiny worms were evolving, gaining in both size and crevice proficiency. In only a few million years they learned to travel the crevices of the universe as readily as those of the material realm. They developed belches that had the force of furnaces and served as weapons of aggression. Finally they grew to massive size and came to govern any wormholes they chose. Other travelers learned to avoid them.

But some others fought back, clearing regions of Worms. That was annoying. In the course of further eons the Worms developed countermeasures that were increasingly effective. The normal Worm had no need of intelligence beyond a minimal level, but there came to be a superior mother Worm who, if not actually smart, had other abilities that compensated. Such as

HAIR PEACE

perceiving the nexi of space/time, those critical points where reality itself could be modified if correctly nudged. She was Wonder Worm, and she labored assiduously to forward the Worm interest by touching a nexus to alter the reality of any competing culture.

Quiti, Gena, and Orchid drew back and consulted. "The Worm raid on the embassy—to eliminate us?"

"That's too crude," Gena said. "That's just blasting away physical structures."

"Why do they bother," Quiti asked. "Why be crude, when they can touch a nexus and eliminate us without a trace of our ever existing?"

"Excellent question," Orchid said. "Maybe changing reality is complicated and fraught with unintended side effects, such as the possible elimination of friends and allies, so they do it only as a last resort. For most purposes, a Worm raid suffices."

Gena and Quiti nodded. That did seem to make sense.

"But now that we have anticipated the Worm raid, and done some spot research of our own so as to learn of Wonder Worm, it won't be long before she catches on and comes after us. We could soon be in trouble."

The fabric of space/time shivered around them. A monstrous figure appeared, of a Worm six feet in diameter and long in proportion.

"Uh-oh," Gena said. "I think we're in trouble *now*."

"In our own dream?" Quiti asked. "How can that be?"

The Worm's snout dilated. Devastating energy shot out.

They vacated without thinking, as the space around them fried.

It was definitely now.

CHAPTER 10: PEACE

They woke in the Embassy back on Earth.

"What just happened," Quiti asked, "And how did it happen?"

"We vacated our dream, to save our hides," Gena replied. "But my question is, how did Wonder Worm get inside our dream? It should have been private."

"Worse," Orchid said. "She knows our home base, here, and will come after us here next."

"She must be tracking our mental presence," Quiti said. "If she wipes out our minds, we're done for."

"So we had better get our minds the hell away from here," Gena said.

"And go where?" Quiti asked. "That she can't track us as fast as we can go?"

"Maybe not," Gena said. "Follow me." She dived back into the dream.

They followed her, and found themselves at—
"The Sorceress' Castle!" Quiti exclaimed, recognizing the environs. For there was the walled castle with its front portcullis, just as it had been when they played out their fantasy story of three princesses.

"Take it, Quiti," Gena said. "She's your friend."

Quiti went to knock on a bar of the portcullis. "May we enter?"

The hulking werebitch guard peered out at her. "Princess Quiti! What are you doing here?"

"It's a long story. I think we need to see the Sorceress."

The guard hesitated, because although the Sorceress normally saw nobody, Quiti was a special case. She had taught the denizens and the Sorceress herself how to be vastly more appealing to males. That counted for a lot.

The Sorceress appeared. "Aren't you out of context, Quiti? We're merely on standby here, awaiting our next fantasy adventure. I maintain the castle as a private retreat, as I like it."

"My friends and I are on the lam," Quiti said. "We are trying to hide." She indicated Gena and Orchid.

"Seriously?"

"Deadly. We are in a joint dream state, but our business transcends our present state. We need your help, but must warn you of the danger."

"A dream! I thought there was something odd about this setting. I was taking a nap, and found myself here."

"This is to normal dreaming what whales are to minnows. It's a joint effort, a shared dream, making a new reality. We brought you into it, and you are bringing your minions into it with you. Can you help us hide?"

The Sorceress hardly paused. She was a competent organizer. "It is easier to get lost in a crowd,

HAIR PEACE

whether dreaming or waking. I will arrange a distraction."

"Thank you."

The Sorceress raised her voice. "Girls, we are about to have a blowout party. Signal the Sorcerer to bring his minions on a panty raid, contents included. Rape will be impossible." Then a message to her own minions: "Uniform of the day is panties, nothing else. You have minutes to organize your roles and make yourselves pretty."

Panties with contents? That meant female bodies. Rape impossible? That meant the girls would cooperate fully. A sexual orgy was incipient.

"That's some distraction," Gena murmured appreciatively.

"The emotional noise will be phenomenal," Orchid said.

"It will be impossible to distinguish three specific visitors in such a melee," Quiti said.

"Exactly," the Sorceress agreed. "We will have emotional privacy."

The ladies of the castle scrambled to comply. Actresses all across the galaxy roused themselves or put themselves to sleep to fill familiar roles of a roughly humanoid nature, though they themselves were of entirely different species. Some were fish, some insects, some unclassifiable by any Earthly means. In their roles as zombies, vampires and werewolf bitches they got into panties (and nothing else) and disported themselves on beds, where they brushed fur, cleaned skin, arranged tresses, and applied makeup. They were ready for action.

Quiti had to admit they looked sexy as hell, despite or perhaps because of their fantasy natures. The zombies had heavy makeup, the vampires kept their mouths closed, and the werewolves stayed mostly in their human bitch forms. All were well endowed, as their minimal outfits revealed, and seemed about to burst out of their panties. It was clear that they liked this type of acting, doing things that were forbidden or unknown in their natural states. Indeed, rape was impossible.

Meanwhile, Quiti knew the Sorcerer was similarly marshaling his own humanoids: dwarves, giants, elves, trolls, goblins, ghouls and others. They would soon be marching on the castle with banners (or "whatever") erect.

The Sorceress led the three of them into her private chambers. "Now we can talk. I know Quiti and Gena, but not you, Ghobot lady."

"She is Orchid, the mother of the lost Ghobot child I told you about," Quiti explained. "We have formed a Trio. Now we are in trouble."

"This should be interesting," the Sorceress said appreciatively. She liked interesting things; it was one reason she had become a galactic actress.

"I have a question," Orchid said. "If everyone else but us are into wild sex, won't the contrast be obvious? We may only attract attention we don't want."

"Excellent point," the Sorceress said. "Yet it is difficult to have a serious discussion while engaging

HAIR PEACE

wildly, and while I would be happy to make out with the Sorcerer, who is a delicious hunk, and there will be a number of males who would enjoy ravishing your bodies with or without your attention, you three I suspect are not eager to indulge with other than your chosen partners."

The three exchanged a look. The Sorceress was exactly on target. They liked being sexy, but only with their loving partners.

"However, there may be a workaround," the Sorceress continued after a fraught moment. "Suppose I make the walls transparent, so that the visiting males not otherwise occupied can see us plainly without being able to get inside? We could tease them a little. They might be quite interested, and their emotions would be loud."

Quiti laughed. "What a tease! I'm for it."

"Teasing is satisfactory," Gena agreed.

"We Ghobots make a specialty of it," Orchid agreed.

The walls became transparent. The four of them stripped down to their panties and primped, or appeared to; their costumes simply adapted. This, too, promised to be fun.

The males arrived. Almost immediately a motley collection of humanoids clustered outside the chamber, peering in. Quiti performed her Hair Dance, complete with invisible legs under the skirt. Gena swung her hips and bounced her bosom in a manner Quiti had not seen from her before. The Sorceress did a dance of her own, her legs fully visible and utterly sexy. But Orchid's dance eclipsed the others. It was immediately apparent that she had not exaggerated when she said it was a specialty. Even Quiti, a completely heterosexual woman, was fascinated by the glimpses she got. Suddenly she was eager to get home and haul her husband Roque into bed, if they even bothered with a bed.

And the humanoid males simply paused and stared. They might stem from all manner of alien creatures, but their roles attuned them to humanoid sex appeal, and this was the quintessence of that. As teases went, this was the ultimate.

The Sorcerer appeared, having gotten his troops organized and assigned in record time. The Sorceress blew him a kiss and signaled that he should take another girl or three instead; she would join him later. He seemed glad to oblige, knowing that she would in due course make those others seem like amateurs.

Then, while the panty raid got into full swing in the rest of the castle, and the raw passions suffused the mental environment, and the watching males stood drippingly transfixed, they talked, updating the Sorceress on what they were doing.

"Serious business indeed," the Sorceress agreed as she mooned the ogre who was orienting on her. He practically fell over in a swoon. "I had not known of Wonder Worm before, but I certainly appreciate the danger she represents to you. But we can't maintain this party indefinitely. WW will track you down the moment the surrounding passions fade, as they soon will. She must already have caught on that you are in here somewhere. You will need to be ready for her."

HAIR PEACE

"They soon will fade," Quiti agreed morosely as she flashed an eager goblin with a high kick. "But we need more time to work this out."

"That can be arranged," Orchid said as she inflated her breasts under the nose of a drooling satyr. He grabbed for her involuntarily, his hands slapping ineffectively into the glassy wall.

"How?" Gena demanded desperately as she made as if to kiss a troll. His lips smacked the wall, but he hardly seemed to notice.

"Announce the second round," Orchid said. "The males having expended their initial rounds will become quiescent. But the females can be challenged to rouse their partners to a second performance. Only when they succeed will the game be considered finished. That is likely to take longer than the first round, but the males should be happy to cooperate, and the emotions will continue to surge."

The Sorceress acted immediately. "Attention, girls. When your partner or partners finish, it becomes your challenge to rouse them to a second performance. The last to climax her partner has to wash the pots tonight." Not that there were dirty pots in a fantasy dream castle, but the threat was in the spirit of the enterprise.

There was a new stir outside as the girls got on the challenge. Meanwhile the four continued dancing and talking.

"This Wonder Worm," the Sorceress said. "How is it I have not heard of her before? A creature as powerful as she is should make galactic waves."

"It seems she does not much like publicity," Orchid said. "She is trying to snuff us out so we won't expose her machinations."

"Has she done this before, elsewhere?"

"We don't think so."

"If someone messed with her before, and she snuffed that person out, shouldn't there be a record? There are galactic record keepers, such as the Encyclopedia Galactica, or Galactopedia, as well as the Wormpedia. They are quite thorough."

"I am familiar with them," Orchid said. "There is no reference to WW."

"Don't you find that odd? You can hardly be the first she has gone after."

"Well, if she eliminated them by unhappening them, as we hope to eliminate the Worm raid on Earth—"

"There would be no record," the Sorceress concluded. "There could have been a hundred prior cases, all eliminated before they happened. Just as you will be eliminated if she catches you."

The three women stared at each other. Of course that was it!

"But what can we do about it?" Quiti asked, chagrined.

"You will have to beat her at her own game. Unhappen *her.*"

"But she derives from eons before our time. We saw that."

"Because you went there, in your dream," the Sorceress said. "That's where she saw you. That

HAIR PEACE

suggests that you do have the potential. That's why she is after you. You need to realize that potential, and take her out before she takes you out, literally."

Again, the three stared at each other. "We sought ultimate enlightenment," Gena said. "This is something less than that, but maybe it is what we need."

"Needing it is one thing," Quiti said. "Achieving it is another."

"But the alternative may be our own elimination," Orchid said.

"So we'd better figure it out," Gena said. "Our very existence depends on it."

Quiti remained bothered by details. "If she can eliminate us by going into the past and unhappening us before we ever get going, and now she knows that's what it will take rather than a simple blast in our future, why is she chasing us now?"

"Good question," Gena said. "She's doing it the hard way. There must be a reason."

"You say she's not smart," the Sorceress said. "That might be a key."

"Maybe so," Gena said. "I am thinking of a flower garden with weeds. You want to take out the weeds without hurting the flowers. You don't mow it all down at the outset; you isolate a weed and carefully pull it out, leaving the neighboring flowers intact. It's tedious, but it does the job."

"We're weeds?" Quiti asked.

"In her garden," Gena agreed. "So she's out to catch us and remove us without disturbing anything important."

"That looks effective from here," Orchid said. "Is there a smarter way of doing it?"

"There had better be," Quiti said. "And we had better find it in a hurry."

"In my garden," Gena said, "I tried to use more general ways to eliminate weeds, because I had to leave the garden unattended for days at a time while I drove my rig on a delivery, and because doing them all by hand gave me a sore back. Prevention, such as layering mulch, sometimes spreading weed deterrent that did not affect my flowers. It seemed impossible to get rid of all the weeds, but I could keep it manageable. It seemed to me that I had to be smarter than a weed."

"We're surely smarter than Wonder Worm," Orchid said. "But she is far more experienced than we are. If we do something rash, our inexperience might lead to paradox."

"Paradox?" Quiti asked. "Like going back in time and killing our own grandmother? I should think that would be impossible."

"I *hope* it is impossible," Gena said. "But if we tried something that had that effect, it would surely mess us up even if Grandma survived. Wonder Worm may have run afoul of similar, so now she's more cautious."

"But if we're too cautious," Orchid said, "We're doomed. We may just have to gamble on paradox."

"Maybe not," the Sorceress said.

"Not?" Quiti asked with forlorn hope.

"Two of you are from Planet Earth, and the third has no home planet. The events of the larger galaxy

HAIR PEACE

hardly affect you, as Earth has been socially isolated until very recently. You might do something that entirely disrupted galactic intercourse, and be largely unaffected yourselves. Your isolation becomes a defense against paradox. Wonder Worm, being a longtime creature of the galaxy, has no such protection. You may have a significant advantage."

"That's nice," Quiti said. "If only we knew what to do."

"I am not an expert in time travel," the Sorceress said. "But I understand that some can do it via specialized dreams, as you did when discovering the Worm invasion of Earth. That is evidently what Wonder Worm does. Now she is chasing you in your special dream, the one that I am sharing with you at the moment. I am thinking that you need more than a dream your enemy shares, to prevail against her."

"Oodles more," Quiti agreed.

"There is a legend among our people," Orchid said. "I thought it was mere fantasy, but now I wonder. It indicates that some achieve very special powers via a dream within a dream."

Gena laughed. "Some Earth psychology says that we dream about things that are on our minds, that we suppressed while awake, and that a dream within a dream indicates a suppression that even a regular dream can't handle. Such as a sexual desire for one's mother. I doubt that sort of thing is relevant here."

The Sorceress didn't laugh. "There are species that do breed with their mothers. It's not suppressed knowledge. For our purpose here, it could mean a distillation of your present dream that might grant additional power."

The three gazed at her. "Another level of dreaming," Gena said. "If we can travel somewhat in time in this dream, and perform an act, what might we do in that next level of dream?"

"We might change the Worm's reality," Orchid said.

"And maybe, unhappen her before she unhappens us," Quiti said. "But still, we don't want to face her head on. She'd pulverize us."

"That's where your intelligence comes in," the Sorceress said. "She can't figure out how to eliminate you without first catching you and yanking you out by the roots, or maybe just incinerating you so you can't do her any harm. But if you study the situation, you may be able to get to her origin in the distant past and take her out of the picture."

"Let's study," Quiti agreed. "Are there Galactopedia references to the origin of the regular Worms?"

"There are. However—"

The watching males scattered in panic as a wall of their chamber crashed down. A six foot wide snout appeared. A curl of fire revved up.

Wonder Worm had found them.

The three acted almost instinctively. They grabbed onto each other and zoomed out of the castle, barely avoiding incineration. They might be in a shared dream, but so was their enemy, right there with them.

HAIR PEACE

The Worm followed them, this time refusing to give them any leeway. They were floating above the castle, and it was apparent that the Worm could wriggle faster than they could float. Her dreadful snout was already reorienting.

"That dreamed dream!" Quiti gasped. "Into it! Now or never."

They clasped hands and focused on sleep. If this didn't work, they were doomed.

Wonder Worm expelled a jet of fire right at them.

It passed through them and went on, leaving them untouched.

They were in the dream within a dream. It was a different frame. Their perspective was enormously magnified. They saw the Worm reacting with surprise, no longer seeing them, if seeing was what she did.

"She'll catch on soon enough," Gena said tersely. "Follow her timeline to her origin, before she can react."

They did, seeing it as a vaporous trail into the Worm's past. They followed it at the speed of time itself. It led back to Worm World, eons ago, where the variant that was Wonder Worm was first evolving.

"Make an Amnesia Bomb!" Quiti told Orchid.

"Here it is."

They flew to the moment of the breakthrough, when the special Worm formed. They dropped the Bomb into her gaping maw.

Nothing happened. But that was the point. The Worm had forgotten not the moment but the entire process. She never made the key breakthrough of dreaming.

It was that simple, once they knew what to do.

They reverted to the present. There was the Sorceress's Castle. They entered the central chamber. The Sorceress was not there.

Quiti expanded her telepathy to locate her friend. And found nothing. There were galactic actresses all around, skillfully plying their men, but no Sorceress. Another creature governed them.

"Uh-oh," Quiti said.

"A side effect," Gena agreed. "We Earthlings were protected from paradox, and Orchid too, but not the Sorceress. She was too much a creature of the galaxy."

"Damn damn damn! She was my friend."

"But the paradox affects us," Orchid said, "because it was the Sorceress who gave us both time to consider, and the idea of the distilled dream. Without her we would not have found the key, or at least not in time to save our hides."

"Which means it's not over," Gena said. "This is perhaps a trial run, a showing of our error. Like revisions on a computer screen, we must select what works and does not mess us up, before we do the final save."

"We must go back and revise," Orchid said. "Get it right before we exit the dream state."

"Yes!" Quiti exclaimed, gratified by this reprieve.

They went back to the Worm origin. They discovered they were able to take back the Amnesia Bomb by intercepting their own timeline just before it.

HAIR PEACE

Then they loosed it again, seconds later. Again there was no apparent effect.

They returned to the present, and to the castle.

There was the Sorceress! Quiti flung herself at her, and hugged her closely.

"I gather you had an interesting experience," the Sorceress remarked.

"You were gone!" Quiti exclaimed. "We had to go back and do it over to get the right variant, without that side effect. It worked!"

"I am relieved," the Sorceress said. "I was not aware of the lapse, but find myself a bit nervous in retrospect."

"So is Wonder Worm really gone?" Gena asked.

The Sorceress was puzzled. "Is what gone?"

Because of course they had no longer discussed the Worm, who had never existed in this frame. This was just a fun visit. They had accomplished their mission.

"However," Orchid reminded them, "It is not complete until we exit the dream and fix our chosen reality in place. As yet it is still supposition."

"That's right," Gena agreed. "Just as I dreamed my alternative future, then woke and went to seduce and marry my husband for real. The dream was only a guide."

"That dream," Orchid said. "But our dream within a dream is a version of reality, as we know by the absence of Wonder Worm. We need to emerge from both levels to fix reality."

"We have found the version we want," Quiti said. "Let's get out now."

They held hands while the Sorceress watched. "Focus," Gena said. "Wake!"

"Wake!" Quiti and Orchid echoed, joining the focus.

"However, the Worms have never been more than a nuisance to travelers," the Sorceress said. "I don't see why you are concerned about them now."

The three froze. Had they not emerged?

Then Quiti caught on. "She was speaking when Wonder Worm came, and we dreamed our way out of it."

"We are down a level," Gena agreed.

"Did I miss something?" the Sorceress asked. "To what are you referring?"

The three laughed together. "You may find this hard to believe," Quiti said. "But we just changed reality. Something terrible attacked, and we went into our secondary dream, dealt with it, then returned. No time passed for you."

"I am not sure I—"

Quiti sent her a telepathic parcel covering their dream within a dream.

"Oh, I see," the Sorceress said, amazed, for the parcel could not be doubted. "And I actually vanished in the course of that adventure!"

"We're glad to have you back," Quiti said. "Now we need to exit *this* dream level. We do thank you for your participation; you helped us accomplish what was necessary."

HAIR PEACE

"It seems I did," the Sorceress said, still amazed.

"I will be in touch later in real life," Quiti said.

Then the three held hands again and focused. "Wake!" they said together.

This time they woke back in the Embassy on Earth, in their physical bodies. "I'm relieved to have that done," Quiti said. "Now we have fixed the new reality, and are safe at last from—"

There was a piercing scream from outside. They scrambled out. There was a giant Worm terrorizing passers-by.

"Oh, no!" Quiti breathed, horrified. "We *didn't* change it, and now they're coming for us in the present time!"

"But we *did* change it," Gena said. "This has to be an anomaly."

Quiti grasped at the straw. She reached out with her mind to touch the limited mind of the Worm.

And discovered that it was as confused as they were. Somehow it had gotten on the wrong trail.

"It's lost!" Quiti said. "It was chasing us with the pack, when it was Idola, Flower, and me, and didn't catch the revocation. It's a young Worm, inexperienced. It landed off the Web, the way Flower did, and doesn't know how to return. In fact it was also caught by our elimination of Wonder Worm, who it remembers vaguely as in a dream, so is doubly confused."

"Understandably," Orchid said. "That dream will soon fade."

"Then show the Worm the way back," Gena said. "It should be harmless."

Quiti was not entirely sure of that, but she approached the Worm physically, reaching out to it telepathically. Its deadly snout oriented on her. *Follow me*, she thought strongly, with a motherly nuance. Then she walked to the nearest Web intersection that was large enough for a single Worm. It was, of course, the one it had arrived through, that they had overlooked before; possibly the change of reality had changed the connection also.

The Worm followed.

Quiti stood beside it. *Dive in, and follow your own scent trail back. You will soon find your companions. No need to tell them you got lost.* She was actually mothering a Worm!

The Worm sniffed the crevice. *Thank you, Mother*, it thought gratefully. It dived in and was gone.

Gena caught Quiti before she fainted from relief, and guided her back inside. "There is one more thing we need to settle."

Quiti groaned mentally. "I think I'm too unsettled to settle anything for anyone else. Can it wait?"

"No. We must decide before the children return."

"I think I know," Orchid said. "It frightens me."

Something that frightened the Ghobot? Quiti did not like the smell of that. "What, then?"

"It is this: we three have happened upon the most phenomenal power in the universe. We need to decide how to handle it."

"We do," Orchid agreed soberly.

HAIR PEACE

Quiti stared at them. "What are you talking about? Didn't we just get rid of that threat? Wonder Worm is gone."

"It is the ability to travel in time, as we did before," Gena said. "With the special dream, but into the past as well as the future. And to knowingly change history, via the dream within a dream. Wonder Worm had it to an extent, and misused it. What of us?"

Quiti realized she was right. They had done that. "But we didn't misuse it," she protested.

"Not this time," Gena agreed grimly. "But power tends to corrupt, as we saw with Wonder Worm. Are we incorruptible?"

"We're human!" And Quiti realized that that was the answer: humans were highly corruptible. "Uh-oh."

"But not entirely," Orchid said. "The three of us together are two parts human, two parts Hair, one part Chip, and one part Ghobot. We seem to need to be together to change history."

"Oh, damn," Quiti said. "Do you mean we'll have to separate forever? I hate that; you're my friends." Indeed, their melding had made them most intimate friends. She loved them both.

"I think not," Gena said. "There could be other time travelers. We need to watch, to be sure they don't undo what we have done."

"Just as Wonder Worm watched, for beings like us," Orchid said.

Quiti shuddered. "We don't want her back."

"So I think that means we shall have to stay together," Gena concluded. "To watch the galaxy, and to guard against any corruption, including our own."

"That's one tall order," Quiti said, awed. "How can we be sure we're up to it?"

"We can't ever be sure," Orchid said.

"We may not even be the best prospects," Quiti said. "I'd have chosen more qualified folk."

"We did not choose it," Gena said. "It was thrust upon us. But now it's ours, and we simply have to do our best. We have no choice."

"We have no choice," Orchid agreed.

"No choice," Quiti echoed. "I hope we're up to it."

"Indeed," Gena said. "The welfare of the galaxy depends on it."

But there was one saving grace. "We'll be together," Quiti said.

"That prospect does not dismay me unduly," Orchid said.

Then they laughed, though there was nothing funny about it. That was reassuring in its fashion. They were, after all, laughing together.

"Now let's relax," Gena said. "The others will be returning soon."

"Lotsa luck there," Quiti said. "I'm hung up on the universe."

"The universe will surely survive if we take a nap," Orchid said. "I mean an ordinary nap."

"I'll be disappointed if it doesn't," Gena said with a smile.

HAIR PEACE

Quiti was recovering in the office when the other Hairs and Chips returned from their galactic engagement. Husband Roque hugged and kissed her. "Did we miss anything?" he asked her. "Hope you weren't too bored, stuck babysitting Earth."

"Nothing we couldn't handle, dear," she responded. She could catch him and the others up later. Right now he had the bedroom urgently on his mind, and not for sleeping. She could handle that.

After that, life simplified. Quiti invited the Ghobots to come settle in the Hair Embassy, as all of them could fit in a single room. She spelled out firm rules for their interaction with human tourists, limiting the degree of emotion that they could provide. There would be no addiction. As long as they retained that discipline, they would not be rendered unwelcome. The income from the tourist industry would enable them to build their own Embassy building and fund other worthwhile projects. They could, and should, be a beneficial influence on the planet. That was the ideal.

Meanwhile, Quiti, Gena, and Orchid would start quietly training other Hair/Chip/Human/Ghobot trios for dream duty. They would make sure there were no unpleasant surprises emanating from the galaxy. No Worms in the ointment.

And of course the rest of Planet Earth might never know. As far as it was concerned, there was a neat new tourist industry that was highly enjoyable, but not extreme. Plus a few curious but generally harmless aliens.

The Hair Peace was about to commence.

AUTHOR'S NOTE

This is the third novella of the *Hair* trilogy. The first, *Hair Power*, started with Quiti as a terminally-ill young woman looking for a convenient place to commit suicide. She helped an alien hairball, who gave her what she facetiously asked for: a decent head of hair to mitigate her baldness from chemotherapy. She got more than that. The second, *Hair Suite*, saw Quiti and her companions get into the galaxy via the Wormhole Web, and become a successful entertainment troupe. This third one is just an incident in passing, much of which never actually happened, as you have seen. Who would have thought that rescuing a lost child could become so complicated?

I made the first note for *Hair Peace* on August 9, 2017, and continued making notes on an almost daily basis until I started formal writing on September 6. It moved along okay until the 10th when there was one of those annoying interruptions the mundane world likes to throw at writers. Hurricane Irma, perhaps the most powerful storm ever to originate in the Atlantic Ocean, arrived. Every hurricane orients on us here in Central Florida, but fortunately their eyes aren't very good so they can't see us well and they generally miss. But Irma was one determined girl; she cruised the entire length of central Florida searching for us, her center finally passing about twenty five miles from us. We were by no means the hardest-hit victims, but there were four days of power outage that wiped out much of our carefully frozen food, and eight trees down across our three-quarter mile drive. Clearing those gave me some extra exercise, you bet. We live on our little tree farm, you see. It took another four days after the power returned to dig out from under, as it were, and we didn't get our phone back for two weeks. Finally I resumed typing text on September 18, and continued until end-of-the-month chores and catching up on other backlogged things like reading books and viewing videos caused another nine day interruption. But on October 7, I resumed and continued until the end of the first draft. Then I took a few more days off to let it jell, just in case I had forgotten something important such as a proper conclusion (and I had, but I fixed it, I think), and returned to amend and edit it. So writing even a 33,000 word novella can be an intermittent thing.

Will there be another in the series? I doubt it, as the Hair theme seems somewhat played out, and our Trio is determined to keep the world clear of disaster. It was the first novella done in my new computer system, breaking it in, and breaking me into a new operating system. No, not like the movie *Her*, which I viewed in the last break, where the man falls in love with the lady operating system. No such luck for me. Now I feel free

HAIR PEACE

to move on to other pieces, and to the next Xanth novel.

The title was suggested by my correspondent Sally Allen. I loved it the moment she thought of it. It was proofread and copy-edited to a degree by Scott M Ryan, Anne White, and John Knoderer, three more fans. I expect it to be published by DREAMING BIG, run by Kristi King-Morgan, yet another fan. So you can see I wouldn't be much of a writer without the active support of my fans. My website is www.hipiers.com/, where I have a monthly personal column, information on my novels, and maintain an ongoing survey of electronic publishers with candid feedback from authors who use them. You are welcome to check it out; the site would be pointless if not visited, and I hope appreciated, by fans like you.

www.ingramcontent.com/pod-product-compliance
Lightning Source LLC
Chambersburg PA
CBHW030306130626
46549CB00002B/716